Full Circle

A Journey Of Love, Betrayal And Forgiveness

OGUGUA AJAYI

FULL CIRCLE

Ogugua Ajayi

Full Circle

By Ogugua Ajayi

Cover Design: IfeAdigo
Published by Love Legacy Media

"Trust in the Lord with all your heart and lean not on your own understanding. In all your ways acknowledge Him, And He will direct your paths."

Prov 3: 5-6 NKJV

Acknowledgements

I WANT TO THANK my Father and God for His unfailing love towards me. I pray that the words of my mouth and the meditations of my heart, will always be pleasing to you.

To my husband, Damilola Ajayi. You wouldn't let me give up even when I got tired. Thank you so much for your support. Thank you for being the best friend I could ever ask for. You truly are God's gift to me.

To my lovely Sisters, Joy Iwendi and Chidinma Maduka. Thank you for your unwavering support. With both of you cheering me on, I feel I can do anything. I love you ladies so much.

I would like to thank Ihunnaya Egere-Oranye, Nwakerendu I. Waboso, Oyidiya Elendu, Chidinma Princewill-Chijoke and Anne Chinedum Ekedum. I call you ladies my third eye. God bless you for the constructive critique. You took this story to a whole new level!

Special thanks to the Federal Government Girls College Owerri 93 set, my sisters for life and members of the Victory Christian Fellowship Alumni Group. God has indeed blessed me with you all.

Thank you to all the members of my tribe. Thank you for reading everything I put out. God bless you.

Chapter One

IT WAS RAINING HEAVILY and as Alice expected, the power went out, throwing the room into darkness. Her generator automatically kicked in and the lights came back on. Alice stretched her hand to open the window beside her bed to let in some fresh air.

She sat up on the bed but, feeling too lazy to get down to fetch the TV remote, she grabbed her phone and snuggled under her blanket. Alice sighed.

Just another Friday night with Facebook, she thought.

She flicked through her newsfeed until she stumbled upon a post by a contact of hers, Ugo Nwokedi. A smile creased her lips as she read his post, a comprehensive write-up on the beauty of the Nigerian '*Ugu*' leaf. Ugo went on to educate his audience on the leaf's botanical name, its properties and benefits of the planting processes he had developed. Alice threw back her head reading and laughing, then she rushed over to the Messenger App to chat him up.

"Ugo, the farmer," Alice wrote.

"Hey dear, you are online, too?"

Alice continued. "You are so funny! Is it an ordinary Ugu leaf you are describing like it was your beloved?"

"Lol. There is no greater love than that of one who gives his life for another. The Ugu, the pumpkin leaf, is growing for the sole purpose of providing nourishment to thousands of people. The least I can do is appreciate it for all its sacrifice."

Alice smiled again. "Lol. You are something else. There is only one other person in the universe I know who can match your enthusiasm for God's green earth."

"Really, who?"

"My friend, Uzo, whom I have known since secondary school. She owns a farm in Abuja. Come to think of it, I should introduce you. You know what they say, Aves of a common plumage frolic in close proximity."

"You have lost me there. What do you mean by Aves of a plumage?"

"*Kaii,* farmer boy, can't you decode its meaning? Birds of a feather flock together."

"Ah, that's why I defer to you in English and I stick to farming."

"Anyway, before I go on with this idea, I have never asked but was wondering, are you in a relationship?"

"Ahh, I am waiting for you to go out with me."

Delight spread through her body. She would never even dream of dating a farmer, but being desired was exciting, nevertheless.

Alice stopped to think for a moment and then continued typing. "*Abeg, quit with the jokes, jare.* That will never happen. Let me go through the checklist. Single, check… how old are you?"

"You are breaking my heart, Alice. I'll be thirty - eight in a couple of months."

Alice stared at her phone and grimaced, wishing she had not brought up the topic. Her best friend, Uzo, was not really the cougar type.

"Alice, are you there?"

She quickly resumed typing again. "Yes, I am sorry. Forget what I said."

"No, why should I? Am I too ugly for your friend? How about all of us of a common plumage flocking?"

Alice smiled and shook her head. This guy was just ridiculous.

"My friend and I are forty-one."

"Is that all? When you said she was older, I thought she was sixty or something. The question of age is moot. I only want to meet another farming enthusiast. *Abeg,* can I have her number? Let me greet my fellow bird, so we can frolic."

"Okay, here it goes. I am sending it now. Don't mess me up."

"Relax. I'm a true gentleman."

Alice typed in Uzo's number and hit send.

She chewed her lip, pondering on what she had just done. As usual, she had spoken, or in this instance, written without thinking it through. She had never met Ugo Nwadike in person. He was one of those random 'People you may know' recommendations that popped up from time to time on your Facebook feed.

She remembered the evening, over a year ago on her fortieth birthday. She had decided on a whim to accept all her pending 'Facebook friend requests' and sent invitations to a few 'people you may know', a decision she regretted within 24 hours as her inbox became inundated with absurd requests and weird conversation starters. She embarked on a blocking spree.

She did not block the stranger, Ugo Nwadike. They had hit it off instantly. He made her laugh and they always had a good chat, which was wonderful since it made her lonely weekends a little less lonely. She never imagined he was so young. Maturity oozed each time he chatted. His profile picture was a close-up of his face that did not give much away.

She was not sure how her friend, Uzo, would react to the introduction. She had a good head on her shoulders but was weary of men and their antics. Alice smiled as she switched off her bedside lamp and secured her satin scarf tightly on her head. She could handle any tantrums Uzo may decide to throw. There was a reason they had been best friends for 30 years. Alice knew all the right buttons to press.

Chapter Two

"SWEETHEART DON'T STRESS SO much. I gave him your number because he is a farmer like you. You can never have too many friends in your industry."

Alice had her phone wedged between her head and shoulder as she set up her laptop on her worktable.

"I have never met him in person, just Facebook," Alice said, connecting her earphones. She settled back into her chair. "Uzo, you are overthinking this matter. If you proceed with the chat and get strange vibes, cut it off. *You too dey worry, abeg.*" She laughed and shook her head. "Okay then, let's talk later, love you."

Tope, her colleague, sat three tables away from her, swiveling round in her chair. She stood up, pulled down her tight skirt and strutted across the room in her 6 inches heels, turning the short stretch of office space into a runway. She perched on Alice's desk and folded her arms across her chest. Her pretty mouth turned down in a frown.

"*Alice, so na so you hate me reach?*" Tope said.

"*Wetin dat one come mean this Monday morning? I just dey enter office.*" Alice replied.

"I just overheard you on the phone telling your friend about Ugo Nwokedi."

Alice craned her neck to gauge the distance between her cubicle and Tope's, and her eyes widened.

"*Tope, how your ear take reach here?*" Alice asked in amazement.

"Forget about that. Isn't Ugo Nwokedi the farming industrialist? I understand he is one of the largest producers of palm oil in Nigeria."

"I don't know about that. This is a friend on Facebook. I know he is a farmer but nothing else."

"*Ha, God. I am here o.*" Tope clasped her hands over her chest. "*Other people have and don't even know it. Oya…*"

Tope pulled at Alice's arm, tugging her all the way back to her desk. She flopped down in her chair and switched on her laptop.

"Look, you know I am trusting the Lord for a billionaire husband," Tope said, setting the tone for what she was about to show Alice.

Alice rolled her eyes.

"I have set up a database of every Nigerian millionaire from 35-years old and upwards and categorized them according to their industries."

"Tope," Alice shook her head as the page opened, "on a spreadsheet?"

"My dear, faith without works is dead and information is the new oil. I must be ready for the day I meet my Boaz. Come and see who is at the top of my Agriculture sector list."

Alice peered over her shoulder at the screen and sure enough, there at the top of the list was Ugo Nnamdi Nwokedi. Alice frowned.

"But I never got the impression that…"

Tope slammed her laptop shut and turned to confront a stunned Alice; her mouth curled up in a sneer.

"I thought you were laughing at my list. What I have here is knowledge and wisdom. Well, you have handed one of Nigeria's most eligible bachelors to your friend on a silver platter." Tope gestured in a mock praying posture. "Father God! See me, ready to receive your blessing, but you sent it to someone who does not appreciate it."

Alice returned to her seat and instantly googled Ugo Nwokedi. It was the same person, but not as she knew him. She always imagined him in scrubs, bent over a ridge with a hoe in hand, but on the internet, he was in power suits, making speeches, shaking and mingling with highly influential people. Not a single farming implement or dirt in sight. She struggled over how to handle this new information. What had she done? Had she just passed on an opportunity for her own 'happily ever after' experience? She decided not to give it another thought.

Knowing Uzo, her focus on work and aversion to men, nothing serious would come out of the introduction.

Chapter Three

"SIS, I HOPE YOUR standing invite to come to Lagos for a weekend is still open?" asked Uzo over the phone.

Alice sat up, excitement coursing through her. She switched her phone from her left ear to her right. "Don't tell me madam Busy Bee is finally taking a break to visit me after I have begged for so long?"

"I sure am." Uzo's laughter came loud and clear through the line.

"Wheeee!" Alice bounced on her seat and kicked her legs under her desk in excitement. "You have made my day, Uzo. By the way, *just talk true*, your trip is official, right? I don't want to deceive myself into thinking I am special."

"You are special." Alice heard her friend laugh and imagined her bent over in a fit. Uzo always laughed with enthusiasm.

When Uzo had let it all out and regained her composure, she said, "Well, it's not really work related…"

"What's that supposed to mean? Spill the news, please!"

"Ugo asked me to come over for the weekend."

Alice felt the air leave her lungs in a whoosh. In the last few weeks since she made the introduction, neither Uzo nor Ugo had indicated that they had been in touch, say less of Uzo flying across the country to visit. Indeed, she had been extra friendly in her online chats with Ugo recently, and she thought they were going somewhere slowly. She closed her eyes, trying to shut out the embarrassing thought that they might have been laughing at her behind her back.

"Alice, are you there?"

"Yes, I am here. I had to wrap up a document. Wait, you said Ugo asked you?"

"He has been asking, but this was the first time I could clear my desk and actually come over."

Alice felt like she had swallowed a stone and it settled at the bottom of her stomach.

Uzo continued enthusiastically, oblivious to her friend's mood "I am kinda excited I get to see you, I also-"

Alice cut her off. "A strange guy asked you to come to Lagos and you are packing your bags to come?"

"Well, I just thought after chatting almost every day for a month, it was probably time to meet."

Chatting every day? Alice felt the words like a stab wound in her chest.

"And it was also an opportunity to fulfill a promise I made to my best friend to visit. I thought you would be happy."

"I am not upset. I am just worried for you. Don't you think you are rushing into things?"

"Rushing? To what? I just thought I could come over, meet him in person, and hang out with you as well. Okay?"

"Okay. I really have no problem. Just be careful. I don't want you labeled a gold digger."

"Gold digger, me? Am I begging on the streets? He can feed himself, and so can I."

Alice did not follow up on that. She figured Uzo had not deduced that Ugo was more than capable of feeding himself. It was best she kept mute. Such information might persuade her friend to throw herself at him even more.

"That's fine. I just wanted to give you a heads-up to salvage your reputation. You know, spending the weekend with the guy."

"Stop that, I am spending the weekend with you. It just happens that I will see a guy in the mix. Let's get that clear."

Alice knew she was being silly, but she couldn't help it. She felt betrayed by Uzo. How could she have kept something like this from her for an entire month? Alice would never have done it. Uzo was the first person she called to give all her updates, and she just made it clear Alice wasn't as important to her as she assumed.

As if reading her thoughts, Uzo continued, "I have missed you, Alice, and I didn't want to gist on the phone, due to one thing or another always vying for my attention. I am not using you as an excuse to see him, I am using him as an excuse to see you."

Alice simmered and sprouted a goofy grin.

"Flattery will get you nowhere." They laughed. Apparently, Uzo knew the exact Alice's buttons to press, too. Excitement crept back in her voice.

"So, when are you coming?"

"Are you free this weekend?"

"So soon?" The frown returned, deeper this time.

"Alice. I am not getting that 'I am excited to see my best friend' vibe from you. Is something wrong? Is it work?"

"No… I mean yes… I just have a lot on my plate. But yes, please, come over. I'm looking forward to it."

Alice ended the call and sank into her chair. She glanced in the direction of Tope's desk and caught her intense stare. They were alone in the office. Alice was under no illusion that the just concluded call was a private one.

"So, after all is said and done, you will let Uzo walk in and take over a relationship you cultivated for the past one year."

Alice jerked, but a firm voice in her head reminded her that that the situation was not exactly as Tope painted it.

"Tope, you are messing with my head here. I have never really looked at Ugo that way. Actually, my heart is somewhere else."

"Somewhere else?" Tope was beside her in a blink. *"Oya, gist me, how?"*

Alice shook her head. Tope's proclivity for gossip was legendary.

"Don't laugh o." Alice plucked some fluff off her suit. "But when I gave my life to Christ, I dumped my

unbelieving boyfriend, and that was tough for me. Then one night, while I was crying my heart out to the Lord, I slept off and dreamt a tall, handsome guy had his arms around me and I was gazing up at him. We were talking and laughing. In that dream, I was so happy. It was perfect. Since then, I have looked for that 'something' I felt in my dream. The guy may not be real, but that connection I had with him. I really want that." Alice shrugged. "I don't have that vibe with Ugo."

"Look at this one." Tope's right eyebrow rose to almost touch her hairline. She waved her hand in Alice's face. "Will you snap out of this? What do you mean? You want to give up reality for a dream, a feeling? How do you know the feeling can't develop between you and Ugo, when you haven't given it a chance? Look, I'm not trying to be funny, but I think you've given something great away. If I were you, I would take back my man."

"He isn't exactly my man." Alice turned away.

"How do you know he isn't?" Tope sighed and pulled her ear to emphasize the warning, "You've made this mistake once, don't make it twice. You think your friend Uzo is coming all the way from Abuja to play? Girlfriend, do what you must to correct this. The

Kingdom of God suffers violence and what?…"

Alice slouched in her chair, staring with a vacant expression. Quietly, she completed the quote with a firm resolution. "And the violent takes it by force.'"

AT HOME THAT EVENING, Alice checked her Messenger App to see if Ugo was online. He had been scarce for about a week or so, probably chatting with Uzo. She scowled as the dark thought crossed her mind. Just when she was about to give up, she saw a green circle light up under his name. She quickly shot him a message.

"Hello, Ugo. How are you today? It's been a while."

She waited for a few minutes then he responded.

"Hey, pretty girl. How are you?"

"I'm good. But what kind of friend just disappears from the four corners of the Facebook Earth without checking in?"

"No, don't say it like that. I have been busy and had to set social media aside for a while. I am sorry."

"That's okay. I can see why you've been busy. I heard you single-handedly brought my friend down here all the way from Abuja, something I couldn't accomplish in a year. What magic did you use?"

She read the message twice, making sure it carried the lighthearted tone she intended it to convey and none of her genuine feelings. Satisfied, she clicked send.

"Ha ha. There was no magic. We just both wanted to meet each other."

She felt another stab in her heart.

"Oh, really? You guys clicked that well? Why didn't you tell me you both were getting serious?"

"Well, there isn't much to tell right now. It's been fun. She had a free weekend, and I said why not? Let's get together. I would have made the trip myself, but I can't leave Lagos at this time. She graciously agreed to travel down."

She could not ignore her own disappointment. She had hoped it was all one- sided, but he sounded as if he really wanted her to come. Her irritation with him grew.

"Wait, I hope you are not just playing with her. I know how you guys behave."

"Why would you say that?"

"Because she's older than you. I don't want you to use her as a plaything and dump her."

"Hey, Alice. That's unfair. I never told you her age bothered me. You brought up the age not me and I will not treat any woman disrespectfully."

"Well, I am just warning you. A 42-year-old may not be what you want, you know, with aging looks and potential fertility issues. So, I don't want you to lead her on."

She chewed her lip, wondering if she went too far with the fertility issue statement. She just needed to puncture his excitement a bit. 'Ugo is typing' showed for a long time. She held her breath wondering what his response would be.

"She is going to be 41 and I hear you. Thanks for the advice. I must go now. I guess I'll see you on Friday for the first time."

That was not what she expected, but she knew she could not push it.

"Yeah, Friday, then."

Chapter Four

"IT'S BEEN TOO LONG, my friend," Uzo gushed, pulling Alice into a tight hug. Alice reciprocated. If not for the issue with Ugo, she would have been over the moon. Uzo was not only her friend, she was also like a sister and the closest person on earth to her besides family. She observed Uzo had gained some weight and wondered at the possibility, considering the hours she spent on the farm. But then, Uzo had an undeniably sweet tooth.

"I can't believe I'm here."

"I can't believe it, too." Alice smiled in-between helping Uzo with her tiny suitcase. Both ladies collapsed on Alice's leather couch.

"I love your new apartment. It's beautiful."

Alice grinned with pride, looking around her home, her own little slice of heaven. She had moved to the Lekki area three years ago and spent the first year renting a small one-bedroom apartment at a ridiculous price. It was fortuitous that while handling a client's account, he had told her of his plans to construct residential high-rise buildings that comprised one- bedroom and two-bedroom apartments for the junior executives. Families with children were not encouraged, unless you owned the apartment. The contractor had given Alice a huge discount, and with a loan from her office, she paid the deposit on one of the two-bedroom apartments.

It was simple and elegant. One walked into a single-floor open plan space, with the kitchen area at the far end, leading to a small balcony. Two doors on either side of the kitchen/lounge led to two en-suite bedrooms. She had painted the apartment in a modern color palette of grey and yellow, and ensured the space was clutter free. She had a three-seater leather couch and two wingback chairs on opposite sides with a small glass coffee table in the center.

"Thank you, my friend. My first venture into real estate."

"And I am so proud of you, may it be the first of many." She closed her eyes and clasped her hands like a prayer as she said, 'In Jesus Name.' She opened her eyes and gave Alice a smile and a wink. "By the way, you look well, Alice. Still as gorgeous as ever."

"Gorgeous indeed, yet without a man, and you are traveling cross-country to hook up with one you've never met." Alice pretended to sulk and turn away.

"Well, I have you to blame for that, thank you." Uzo poked her friend's sides, and as expected she buckled in laughter. *"I was on my own, jeje. Na you bring man come."*

The irony was not lost on Alice. "Just don't rush into anything, that's my advice. When people say men are scum, it's for a reason."

"Madam Alice, still as suspicious as ever. I won't rush, I promise." She gave Alice a side hug.

"So, what's the plan?" Alice strolled to the fridge and extracted a packet of orange juice and two glasses from the cupboard.

"Well, the plan is that today I choose where we go, then tomorrow, he decides what we do. Sunday, we do church and then I return to Abuja and prepare for work on Monday."

"Oh, okay, that sounds like a plan, but you don't know anywhere in Lagos." She handed the glass of juice to Uzo.

"I know, I need your help with that. Any recommendations?"

"For your first date?" She could not resist digging as she sipped her drink.

"It's not a date. It's a hangout," Uzo said, raising a pillow over Alice's head and threatening to hit her.

Alice pretended to duck whilst trying to protect her drink from spilling. "Okay, okay," she said, laughing genuinely for the first time since her friend's arrival. "For a first hangout."

"Thank you." Uzo lowered the pillow. "I'm thinking maybe somewhere not too stiff but not fast food either."

"That's a tough one. You know, we single mature woman have a limited crop of places we can go to without looking pathetic."

"Alice, abeg, stop joor."

"Okay, I have heard of a place called Love Legacy café, not far from here, along the Lekki axis. Great food, relaxed atmosphere. You guys can chat and talk without too many disruptions."

"That sounds nice, but wait, the name of the place, Love Legacy? Isn't that too heavy for a non-romantic outing?"

"It's not Love as in lovers. The lady named it after her mum, that's all."

"I guess I can go with that. Can I give him your address?"

"He's coming here?" She frowned, rubbing the nape of her neck and then looked away. "I don't think it's wise, for security reasons. Like we do not know what he is capable of."

"You are right. I didn't think of that. I'll take an Uber and make a judgment call after dinner if I want him to bring me back."

"Much better." Alice sighed in relief.

Alice tried to distract herself. She watched a bit of TV but noticed that all the movies were romantic genres, and she was not interested in that now, not this evening. Her mind kept wandering over to Ugo and Uzo. Were they getting along? Or was it a colossal mess? Alice was ashamed to admit she was hoping for the latter, just so she could have Ugo for herself and see if there was something that could happen between both of them. Around 10 p.m. she sent a text to Uzo.

'Where are you? Lagos is not safe this late. Please, come home. I won't be able to sleep until you get back.'

She did not have to wait long before she got a response.

'Sorry, girl. Leaving now. He's bringing me. See you soon.'

Ugo was coming here! She rushed to have a bath and dress up but tried not to look overdressed since it was late. She hoped to get away with a dash of light lip gloss, especially as using makeup so close to midnight was out of the question.

About twenty minutes later, Alice heard a knock on the door. She smoothed down her tee-shirt and readjusted her denim shorts over her tummy. She opened the door and stopped short. Next to her smiling friend was a huge guy in a suit, who looked nothing like Ugo's Facebook picture.

"Ugo?" she hesitantly asked, stepping back to allow Uzo make her way into the room.

"Oh, no, ma'am. I work for Mr. Nwokedi." He gave a slight bow. "I'm just here to escort madam to the door."

Alice glanced at Uzo, who was beside her grinning like a Cheshire Cat. "Oh, okay, thank you."

"Thank you, Michael." Uzo waved and then dropped her bag on the coffee table.

"Not a problem, madam," he said politely, gave another slight bow and left.

Alice watched him go down the stairs before closing her door. All sorts of questions raced through her head. She swung around to face her friend.

"What is going on? I thought you went to dinner with Ugo. Why are you coming back with Michael? A tall, dark and handsome, Michael, I might add."

"Don't be silly, Alice, Ugo is in the car. He had to take a phone call, so he asked Michael to see me to the door just to be sure I got in safe.

"How rude!" Alice exploded. "I knew he wasn't one you could trust. How can you take a girl out, bring her home and send your staff to see her off without the decency to walk her to the door yourself? That is so inconsiderate. I hope this is the last meeting you are having with him."

"Alice, calm down." Uzo laughed. She dragged Alice to the wingback chair and pushed her down into it. "You have it all wrong. Ugo got a call earlier during dinner around 8:30 p.m. He told the person he would return the call at 10:30 p.m. after we finished dinner. Neither of us thought we were going to stay so long. So, when the person called back, Ugo enquired whether I minded if he took the call because he had committed to 10:30 p.m. He did not want me to wait in the car, so he asked Michael to see me to the door, and he'll come by once the call was over."

"Hmm, so, he is still coming tonight."

"Yes. I hope you don't mind. Just to say good night." She sat on the couch and pulled off her wig, massaging her cornrows with her fingers. She sighed with relief at the freedom. "I did that vibe test and I think he's okay. I promise, I really have a good feeling about him."

"If you say so." Alice shrugged. "So, tell me, how was the evening? And why are you taking off your wig, earrings and co? I thought you said he would come to say goodnight?"

"Alice, we had such a great time this evening, and I feel I have to do this. If whatever is going on has any potential, he should see me as I am as soon as possible. Let him not go home thinking of me as Cinderella." Uzo pushed herself off the chair and picked up her shoes from where she had thrown the pair. "So, the wig is going, makeup is going, jewelry is out and glory to Jesus, this girdle is definitely coming off and I'm changing into my pajamas. Let him come and see what he's up against. At my age, I don't have time to play games."

Alice looked at her friend's retreating form as she left the living room to carry out her plan. She shook her head. Uzo had been like this for as long as she could remember, the only one who never preened for boys in school. She wore makeup on rare occasions and always chose comfort over style. Her laissez-faire attitude in the University had put off quite several guys, but Uzo didn't care. She wasn't your typical beauty, at least not with her large eyes, bulbous nose, and full lips that had a sprinkle of freckles around them. On Alice's insistence, she had agreed to get her makeup professionally done for the evening and the effect was dazzling, making her quite attractive, at least in Alice's opinion. Now Uzo wanted to remove all the enhancements and be herself? Who does that on a first date? How would Ugo respond? She figured if it backfired, it would benefit her and surge her personal agenda forward. Best to keep her thoughts to herself.

"Undress quickly," she called after her friend. "I am dying to hear the gist of tonight's hangout."

"Best come along and listen while I change."

Alice joined her friend in the guest room. She watched Uzo struggle out of her girdle, noting the way her tummy fell out like a split sausage. She wore her Pajama top that did nothing to hide her girth and rummaged through her travel bag for the bottoms.

Alice silently thanked God that she would have to do nothing more about this situation. Uzo was about to make a mess of it herself.

"I think there's something here."

Alice forced herself to concentrate on Uzo's words.

"Something where?"

"I meant with Ugo," Uzo said. "Your mind is straying." She shoved both feet inside her pajama bottoms and jumped, pulling the trousers over her hips. "Really, I'm telling you. We've always had lovely conversations on the phone but talking to him in person was easy and fun. He is not only great to talk to, but also pleasant and quite considerate. You should hear how gently he spoke to the waiter at the restaurant. Also, the way he treats Michael. And then my favorite part was our encounter with Baba."

Alice, sitting with her back turned to Uzo and rolling her eyes as her friend extolled Ugo, turned to Uzo sharply.

"Who is Baba?" she asked. This narration was not going the way she wanted.

"Baba is a beggar we found outside the restaurant parking lot. As we passed him on our way out, he called out to Ugo, 'My son. I hope you enjoyed your dinner. Can I have a little something for myself?'

"I was slightly nervous because of the security concerns around Lagos, but Ugo walked over to him and said, 'Baba. I have just eaten. You should eat, too.' He opened his wallet and generously brought out some five-hundred-naira notes."

"Baba was ecstatic and called Ugo a lot of wonderful names in the Yoruba language. Though Ugo did not understand what Baba was saying, he stood there and good-naturedly received the praise. Before we left, Baba said, 'My son, you and my daughter here will have lots of children, you will…' I started laughing and stopped him from carrying on. Inside the car, Ugo asked, 'What did you just do?'"

"I wanted to correct him. He thinks we are together."

"So? We might get together in the future. Why stop us from having all the children God wants us to have?"

"Through all this, his face was dead serious, but I couldn't stop laughing. Then he said, 'In fact, I am upset. I have decided that we will return tomorrow so Baba can complete his prayer for us. This time, please, respond with the appropriate, "Amen". If there is no future with us together, at least I will have my children, you will have yours. Do you see?"

"Alice. I laughed so hard, ehn." She sighed with a dreamy look on her face. "I knew he was joking, but it made me feel so…, I can't explain it, the way he said it was so full of promise. In one sentence, he told me, I would like to see you tomorrow, and second, the possibility of a future is open."

Alice lifted an eye, her left nostril followed suit.

"Do you really believe all that dribble?" Scorn dripped off each word. "Lagos guys will finish you with raps. Ugo is playing you like a fiddle. He knows you're old and desperate for a relationship. So, he's saying all the right things to get into, you know…"

She turned away and peered at her fingernails.

"Wow, Alice," Uzo whispered. "You really know how to kill a mood. I guess it's due to your concern for me but, please, leave it to me to decide if I'm being taken advantage of or not, okay? He was genuine."

"But how do you know for sure? He may be a player." Alice's voice rose.

Uzo matched her tone. "Then why did you introduce him to me?" Her lips trembled and her voice shook.

"I just wanted you to have a friend who was interested in the same things as you. I did not know you would decide to have something more behind my back. That part was all on you."

Uzo wiped at the tears. "That's okay, Alice. It may all come to nothing, anyway. I will pray about it and if we go out tomorrow, I'll ask the Holy Spirit to open my eyes to the true Ugo, so that I'm not blinded by just one night. You are right. You are a good friend, Alice. Thank you."

The knock on the door saved Alice from a response. Uzo's graceful acquiescence sent a tiny jolt of guilt through her, but she squashed it.

Alice quickly followed her out, curious to meet Ugo in person and see for herself his reaction towards her friend. If he was in any way as good looking as his guard, Michael, Alice knew there would be a problem with Uzo. Her friend opened the door and Alice caught her first glance of Ugo Nwokedi. First thing she noticed was his height. He was short, not short, but the same height as Uzo. Alice had never been into short guys. She always said whomever she married, she wanted to look up to literally. He had bright eyes and bushy brows with closely shaved beard and a well- trimmed moustache. He was not dark enough for her taste. She surmised that one could call him handsome, but she did not feel any butterflies.

"So, Ugo?"

"Yes, Alice… Wow… What a pleasure to meet you." He pulled her into a hug. Alice reciprocated. It was nice having a man's arms around her again and from one so clearly enthusiastic about it. She relished the few seconds it lasted. She could overlook the height, she thought.

"So, this is your face. I knew you were gorgeous based off your profile pictures, but they don't do you justice."

"Ugo, stop, please." Alice blushed and moved aside to let him in.

"Uzo, why are you chasing me way?" he said, walking past Alice.

"Go, joor, I'm not chasing you away." She patted the cushion beside her.

"Well, you are in your pajamas and all your accessories are gone." He smiled, settling down beside her "You are inadvertently telling me it's late and I should hurry and leave".

Uzo launched into her normal fit of laughter that grated on Alice's nerves, but Ugo smiled indulgently and allowed her finish.

"I didn't think of it that way, but that isn't it at all. Can I be honest?"

"Sure, go ahead." He shifted on the couch, moving closer to her.

Alice shook her head violently from behind Ugo. Why was Uzo bent on making her takeover plan so easy? How would one tell a guy you wanted him to see you as you are on the first date? It was too much information, a sign of desperation.

"I took it all off to enable you see me exactly as I am. No more Cinderella, this is me." She spread her hands looking away, her vulnerability seeping through.

Ugo came even closer and caught her hands in his

"As far as I can see, Cinderella just changed clothes, took off her wig and her makeup. She is still right here."

There was silence as he gazed at her. Alice saw it, that thing about Uzo. The way her eyes lit up when she smiled, which she did often, and how her inner goodness shone through, spreading like a shower, and touching everyone around her. There was also her astounding confidence in herself and her abilities that made people notice her. All these made her mundane features glow and even intimidate Alice with her conventional beauty.

Uzo broke the silence. She asked, still smiling, "So, er, are we still on for tomorrow?"

Ugo came alive instantly. "Is that a question? Of course! We have unfinished business, remember?" He grinned and gave a cheeky wink. Uzo's glow deepened.

Alice felt a deep stab of envy as she observed them. Could this have been me? She wondered. Could we have had this kind of connection if I wasn't so foolish? Would he have been gazing at me with that look of admiration?

"I better get going," he said finally. Alice released a sigh of relief and saw him out of the apartment.

"So, what do you think, Alice?" Uzo rubbed her palms together, waiting for a response.

"Well, he's saying all the right words. I still don't know what it is about him, but I don't trust him a hundred percent, but you do, obviously." She eyed Uzo's dreamy look.

"It's worse. Alice, I think I'm falling hard and fast."

"Woah there, easy, my friend. This is day one. Let's decide if you're falling hard and fast after day two."

"I just feel as if I've known him forever. You know when you're with someone and it just feels right."

Alice did not know. Her mind went briefly to the man in her dreams, but she pushed that aside. Like Tope said, this was reality.

"See the way he reacted to my explanation about Cinderella. Can you make that kind of thing up?"

"Yes! Writers do it all the time," Alice snapped with a snide look.

"Be a party pooper if you like. But I'm telling you, Alice. If tomorrow goes as well as today and this guy calls me on Monday morning, just know that I'm officially gone. Don't worry, she continued, seeing Alice appalled look, "if he breaks my heart, it was my choice. I am a big girl."

"That's okay, but just don't fall too fast or give in too quickly. I don't have a good feeling about him. He's too sweet, too good, everything is too perfect. Be careful, you know that saying, 'if it's too good to be true...?'"

"I know, I know, mother hen." Uzo came over to the kitchen counter and hugged Alice. "Thanks for watching out for me. Good night. I love you."

Chapter Five

NEXT DAY, AFTER THEY spent the morning shopping and lounging, Uzo announced that Ugo would pick her up for 3 p.m.

"What kind of dinner are you having at three o'clock in the afternoon?" Alice paused mid-way sorting her shopping and studied her friend with a quizzical expression.

"He wants me to tag along to a few of his hangouts. Then he plans to show me around Lagos."

"If you wanted me to show you Lagos, I would have, but I see I am just your accommodation. This visit has nothing to do with me." She left her and went to the living room to flick through TV channels. Uzo dropped the new clothes she was trying on and hurried out of the room to join Alice.

"Don't be like that, don't be angry." She tried to peck Alice, who warded her off with a wave of her arms. "The next trip, I promise, will be just you and I."

"Well, I might not be available for a next time. My beau and I may be busy."

"In that case, I say hallelujah!" Both ladies laughed, the tension quickly forgotten as they watched television together.

When Ugo's car drove into the compound at 2:55 p.m., Uzo was ready and practically flew out of the house.

ALICE BUSIED HERSELF WITH deliverables from work. She went for her church prayer meeting, returned home and cooked. By 8 p.m., she had nothing else to do. The thought of her friend somewhere probably having the time of her life with Ugo amplified her loneliness.

Alice's apartment faced the complex entrance gate, granting her the vantage view of cars entering the compound. She heard a car drive in around 10 p.m. and lifted the curtain's edge. Under the floodlights, a black

SUV with tinted windows parked in her visitor's parking spot. The occupants of the car did not alight. Uzo finally knocked on the door at quarter past eleven.

"Madam, big girl. Which one be all this midnight waka? Is this the proper behavior for a Christian woman?"

"Mummy Alice, relax!" Uzo pulled her into a tight hug. "I insisted he should bring me home early because I didn't want you to worry. Instead, one thing led to another, and we just kept on talking about this and that." She paused and drew Alice into another hug that lingered. When she let Alice go, her eyes brimmed with tears.

"Hey," Alice said, her voice softening. "What's this all about? Did he hurt you?"

"Hurt me? No, Alice, I am just overwhelmed. God bless you for introducing me to Ugo. He is everything I've ever wanted in a partner."

Alice moved out of Ugo's reach, disappointment coursing through her.

"That's what you want in a partner? Really, as short as he is?" Alice knew she had crossed the line, but she couldn't help it.

"Short? He's of average height."

"But you are taller than he is."

"Only when I'm wearing heels. Besides, even if he came in a shorter package, I will still be all over him. I am beyond just looks. He is a wonderful human being."

"Mmm, so what did Mr. Wonderful do today?"

"We had a lovely time. He took me to his apartment. Hey, don't give me that look, nothing happened. I told you I'm on the straight and narrow. He cooked for me and then we just drove around town talking about life, his family, his retired parents in the East and siblings living abroad. Then we talked about my mum, our industry. Dinner was at the same Cafe. He was serious about meeting Baba again so the old man could complete his prayers."

"And how did that go?" Alice forced the words through her teeth. She wanted to slap the sappy look off Uzo's face.

"That was the icing on the cake for me. He recognized us immediately, greeted us warmly and exclaimed, 'Ah, my son and my daughter. I'm so happy to see you again. Did you eat well?'"

"'Yes, we did, Baba,' Ugo said. 'I also want you to have a splendid dinner as well.' And he was generous indeed. Baba thanked him non-stop and this time it was Ugo who stopped him."

"'Baba remember last night, you were praying for me and this woman here interrupted you. Please, today we want you to pray for us fully with no disturbance.' Can you imagine? This silly man pinched my arm."

From Uzo's look, Alice concluded it was an extremely pleasurable pinch.

"'My son, I will pray with pleasure.' And Alice, he prayed we would be happy, that our home will be happy, he even blessed our children.'" Uzo shyly hid her face behind her hands. Alice feared she was going to throw up.

"We held hands and kept saying "Amen" to every prayer. There was something so spiritual about the experience. Then when Baba shifted to praying against evil forces that will try to harm us, I lost it. You know how I feel about the loss of my dad. Standing there, Ugo and I holding hands, hearing the old man pray for us, it was as if my father was praying for us. I was so overcome with emotion that I hugged Baba. "

Alice drew back. "I thought you said this man is a beggar."

"I didn't think about that. In that moment, he was a father figure blessing me. It felt like God was blessing Ugo and I, and it just connected with me.
Ugo held me tight till I was okay and explained why I was so emotional."

"Uzo, you need to snap out of this. You feel you now have the blessing of your late father and the blessing of Almighty God on this thing you have with Ugo? We don't even know what the thing is yet." Alice suddenly panicked. This was getting serious way faster than she thought. She felt herself loosing grip on the situation.

"I know it sounds silly but that's how I felt. As for Ugo, I have melted like butter in the sun. If this guy tells me to jump, I will ask how high."

"Hey!" Alice's shock was genuine. "Can it be that sudden?"

Uzo's eyes took on a dreamy quality. "I don't know how it is for everybody else, but I will not delude myself."

"What makes you think he feels the same way? Did he say anything?"

Her face fell a smidgen. "No, he didn't, not in straight up terms, yet everything is pointing-"

Alice cut her off with a snap of fingers in her face. "Just forget it. That is a sign of a non-committal person. If the evening was as sure-fire, destiny changing for him as it was for you, why didn't he say something? Uzo, easy on this one. I have a bad feeling about this."

She rose and left the living room. She did not want her friend's crestfallen expression to shake her resolve.

49

Chapter Six

ALICE WOKE UP ON Monday morning with a heavy heart. She had awoken earlier to see Uzo off. An Uber took her to the airport. She had moved her trip by a day because Ugo had asked her to. After church service, they had spent the rest of the day together till evening. Alice was in bed when her friend returned, unable to bear another night of gloating about the wonders of Ugo.

Once she left, Alice tried to go back to sleep but kept tossing and turning, multiple thoughts running through her head.

How could life be so unfair? Why would Uzo be on the verge of a 'forever after' and not her? This was not how the script was supposed to play out. For as long as she could remember, she was the one the guys always flocked to. Since she became a Christian, they were not flocking so much, or they didn't pass her vibe test. She wondered if she would die an old maid, but she remembered her dream and how she felt with the guy in it. She reassured herself there was love somewhere out there for her. Maybe Tope was right. Why should she simply roll over and give up? Besides, good things happen to people who fight for it, right?

She stepped out of the shower, determined to do something about it. Uzo had hinted that Ugo had a busy day today. So, he may not be in touch soon. This was her opportunity to derail this speeding train. A plan already formed in her mind. She knew one thing about Ugo. He was deeply superstitious and came from a polygamous home with its attendant problems. His mother raised him to avoid anything that appeared vaguely suspicious and keyed it all to a relative with ill intentions trying to destroy him. He had told her that till this moment, after giving his life to Christ, he still struggled with the fear. Alice smiled. She could work with that.

"HELLO, WHO IS THIS?"

Alice scowled. He did not even have her number saved, even after coming to her house for three days. She had saved his, the minute Uzo gave it to her.

"It's Alice, how are you?" She rushed on before he could respond. "I was wondering, can we meet for coffee somewhere, if you have the time this afternoon."

"I'm at work, Alice, and I have a packed schedule."

She stared at her handset and frowned. Why was he sounding so testy?

"It wouldn't be long. This isn't a casual meet up. It's important you hear what I have to say. It's about Uzo."

"What? Is she okay? She should have arrived by now. I tried calling, but her phone was still switched off."

Good, Alice cheered silently, wiping the irritation that surfaced from his concern over her friend. "She is fine, I think it's better you don't speak to her till we have talked."

UGO WISHED HE HAD not picked the call. Now he could not concentrate. He kept checking his watch till it hit 11 a.m. when he left his office with enough time to get to the spot Alice had picked, a small and quiet coffee bar. Despite his elaborate plans, Lagos traffic did its thing. He arrived ten minutes late, looking harried.

He spotted Alice at once, seated at a corner table. She waved him over, dressed in a corporate navy-blue suit and a yellow and blue scarf around her neck. Her braided hair was perfectly coiffed to the side of her head. He rushed over, anxiety causing him to forget his manners.

"What's the matter, Alice? What's up with Uzo?"

"Will you relax, Ugo? Have a seat and, please, stop hovering."

He let out a deep breath to calm himself. After he took off his blazer and hung it at the back of the chair, he sat down.

"Would you like anything to drink?" She waved for a waiter.

"No, I-. okay, maybe a cup of coffee. Black, please," he said to the waiter, who had quietly appeared at his side. "I need to get back to work. What is it? You made it sound mysterious and urgent."

"I'll cut to the chase then." She clasped her hands on the table and leaned forward. "What I am about to say is difficult but necessary." She bit her bottom lip, thrust out her chin and continued. "I sort of got the impression that you guys really hit it off this weekend."

"Yes, we did. It was great." Ugo could not stop himself from gushing. "Uzo is amazing, just so-"

She cut him off abruptly "That's okay, Ugo, I know you're a Christian. And I know you wouldn't want anything to disturb your spiritual life."

"I don't understand."

"When I introduced both of you, I didn't think you guys will get this serious. I thought I was just introducing friends, but if you are thinking of taking this to another level, perhaps you should listen to me first."

He adjusted in his chair and pushed his coffee cup away from him. "Okay, what's going on?"

"Ugo, I've known Uzo since we were in secondary school. She lived in the town my boarding school was located. Her family was notorious in the area."

"Notorious for what?"

"How do I say this?" She looked around and lowered her voice. "Violent insanity runs in her family."

"Excuse me?" Ugo did not hide his disbelief.

"Calm down. I am not making this up. I have seen her father rampage naked around the town. No one could hold him down. I heard his father before him showed the same traits. I am afraid Uzo may have the same tendencies. "

"Which Uzo?"

Alice looked at him. "This is difficult for me to talk about. But while we were in school, her father was not the only topic of discussion around town. She suffered fits of terrible temper. Once, she took a cement block and broke it over our Social Prefect's head."

"What?" He sat up, finally paying attention.

"Yes, she was angry and struck him repeatedly on the head with a cement block. The poor guy almost lost his life. What kind of anger leads one to do such a thing if you are normal or right in the head?" Alice sensed he was taking her seriously now. He couldn't look her in the eyes and his forehead had a permanent crease. "She behaves well most of the time, but who knows when the illness can rise again? Even if she hides her episodes, who is to know if it will pass on to her children?"

Ugo looked up, his eyes wide.

"You may be too sophisticated to understand this kind of thing, but we should never take spiritual things at face value. You've got to be careful about getting involved with family that has anger and madness in the mix. It never bodes well."

Ugo felt a chill crawl up his spine.

She stood and picked her yellow bag from the chair at her side. "I thought I should let you know before you make that call."

Alice saw the fear in his eyes. "Good," she thought, "Now run!"

She left a deeply reflective Ugo staring into his coffee cup.

Chapter Seven

IT WAS NOT UNUSUAL for Alice and Uzo to go without talking or chatting for days due to their busy and sometimes conflicting schedules, especially when Uzo spent days at her farm. Alice knew she could get away without talking to her for a while, but by the end of the week she was desperate to know if the seeds she planted had borne fruit.

Alice no longer struggled with guilt over what she did. She had succumbed to the voice that justified her actions and allowed it to grow louder, until it convinced her that Uzo was getting what she deserved, a karma for stealing her man and that she, Alice, was the wronged party. She sent a text.

'Hey, girlfriend. How are you doing? How's it been settling back to work?'

Ten minutes passed before she got a reply.

'It's okay.'

That did not sound positive. Alice took a deep breath and typed.

'Is that all you're going to say?'

When she didn't reply, Alice called. After two rings, she picked up.

"What's going on?"

"I am fine." Uzo's voice sounded muffled.

"You don't sound fine, are you ill?"

Uzo did not reply, but Alice could hear a sharp intake of breath and imagined her crying. She retrieved her file from her bag and proceeded to file her nails, waiting for Uzo's response.

"Alice" she said, eventually. "I feel so crushed."

"I don't understand. What's the matter?" She stopped filing her nails, and then remembered Uzo couldn't see her. There was no need to pretend she was interested in what she had to say. She put her phone on speaker and returned to her nails.

"Have you heard from Ugo?" Uzo asked.

"No. I haven't. Not since that Friday evening we saw at my house." The lie easily flowed off her tongue.

"Well, he hasn't contacted me either." Joy flowed through Alice. "I know you told me not to build castles, but I really thought we had something special."

Alice heard more heaving and went back to her nails.

"I have been calling and texting, worried that something might have happened to him. Then I went on Facebook and saw he had made a post publicizing his upcoming charity event. I gave up after that. I had seen for myself that he was alive and well." She stopped to blow her nose. "Before then, I was so sure something was wrong; it was so unlike him to ignore me like that. That's the worst part, the silence. All I can say is that I blame myself, because you warned me. I didn't listen. So, I guess I deserve whatever I get."

Alice listened to her soft cries and decided she should probably say something.

"Don't be so hard on yourself. You wanted to fall in love; he just didn't feel the same way about you."

Uzo went into a full-blown meltdown.

"Stop crying, please. Move on. He is not worth it. Besides, there might be someone else perfect for him, and someone else perfect for you just waiting around the corner."

Alice waited for Uzo to pull herself together and was relieved when the sobs subsided. She had a lot of work to do. She had achieved the purpose of this call. Her plan had worked, and that was all that mattered. Uzo's emotional state was not her concern right now.

Finally, Uzo could speak. "You are right, I had just been blocking the idea of him from my mind, but when you asked just now, all the emotions poured out. I'll be okay."

"Good, that's the attitude. It's weekend, go down the street to Mama Banke's house, organize yourself some nice pepper soup and a chilled coke. Forget about Ugo. He doesn't deserve your tears."

"Alice, please don't make me laugh."

"Why shouldn't you laugh? You are not the first person to have feelings for the wrong person. Did you kill someone? No. Pray about it and leave it in God's hands. He says you should trust Him with all your heart, and he will direct your path. This may be part of His direction."

"Thank you, my friend. You are always so supportive. I will change my perspective about it. Thank you."

"What are friends for? Take care, sweetheart. I'll be in touch. Bye."

When she disconnected the call, Alice punched the air and did a little tap dance. Now that she had gotten Uzo out of the way, it was time to get her man.

She put a quick call to Tope and told her the game plan. Tope dropped a few suggestions and by the time the call ended, Alice was satisfied the scheme was fail proof.

Chapter Eight

UGO WAS NOT MAKING things as easy as Alice had planned. He ignored all her messages on WhatsApp and Facebook Messenger. She was getting frustrated. Two weeks later, she was still checking Facebook regularly for any sign of activity from him. She finally got lucky on a Saturday evening whilst in bed. He made a post on Facebook and was replying to comments. Sleep vanished as she quickly made a comment and then sent him a direct message.

'Ugo, the farmer. Why are you ignoring me? I thought we were friends.'

He replied within a minute. 'Hey Alice. I'm not ignoring you. I've been really busy.'

'You've been busy before and I've never had this kind of attitude thrown at me. Is there a problem? Did I do something wrong? I thought we were close enough, and you were mature enough to handle the truth.'

'It has nothing to do with that. I have moved on.'

Alice kicked her legs in the air, rolled back on her stomach and continued typing.

'That's good. Do you know what? To prove to me there are no hard feelings, let me take you out for dinner. Tomorrow is Sunday, and you can't say you are at work.'

'Alice, I would rather not.'

'I won't take no for an answer, that is if you want peace. This Lagos will not be enough for both of us if you refuse.'

There was a pause and Alice relaxed when his message came in.

'Okay, fine.'

'That's my guy. It's my treat, so don't worry about anything. Send your address and I'll come get you tomorrow around 5p.m.'

"If you insist."

ALICE TOOK HER TIME the next day in choosing an outfit. She dressed intentionally in a fitted single shoulder, knee-length, pale pink dress with edgy silver hoop earrings and heels. She had been to the salon to have her hair wrapped into a bun. Now she added silver accessories round it. She did not need a girdle or body shaper to cinch her waist. She had a body women envied on a regular, and she knew it. At 41- years- old, she looked like she could compete in a pageant alongside young girls and give them a run for their money. She pursed her lips at her reflection in the mirror, taking time to admire the smoothness of her warm brown skin that shimmered from her oval face down to her shoulders, then her gaze lowered to her toned arms. After one more look of approval, she stepped out.

Her confidence was at an all-time high as she drove to Surulere, the part of town Ugo lived. She could not understand how he still stayed in this side of Lagos, when the other big ballers had houses in Ikoyi, Victoria Island, or at least the Lekki Axis. She drove into his compound and saw him leaning against a car with his arms crossed. The frown plastered on his face effectively burst the bubble that encased her since leaving her house. She had hoped they would spend some time in his apartment before they headed off to the restaurant. She parked her car and as he approached, her heart plummeted even further. He had on a pair of jeans and a check button-down shirt. Not exactly the outfit for a romantic dinner. He did not seem to have put in any effort at all.

UGO GOT INTO THE car and her heavy perfume hit him square in the face. He gave Alice a cursory glance.

"Oh, I didn't realize it was a dress- up thing."

"Oh no, it's not." She looked away and spoke animatedly. "I just like to put my best foot forward whenever I have the opportunity. I don't go out much. So, the few times I do, I go all out. So, don't worry, all this is for me, not you."

"Oh, good. If you don't mind then, I really don't want to change."

"You don't have to, let's go." She flipped her head nonchalantly.

He silently thanked God. He had been bashing himself all day for allowing himself get roped into this outing. He did not feel like being social.

When he saw the familiar building of Love Legacy Cafe, his heart sank.

Not here, God, no, he thought. All his emotions for Uzo came rushing through his body.

"Isn't there anywhere else we can go?"

Alice either did not hear or chose to ignore his question. She focused on getting a good parking spot.

"Alice, can we go somewhere else, please?" Beads of sweat formed on his upper lip.

"Why? Don't you like this place? The food is great. That's why I recommended it to Uzo." He visibly stiffened and she turned to him, "Oh, I'm sorry, I didn't know you were so into her like that. It's just a restaurant."

"No… no, I'm not that into her, I just…." He stopped and wondered at the lie that passed through his lips. He just what? Missed her so much that the mere mention of her name set his heart racing. The past month without her had him listless and wandering about the actual essence of life. Now, coming here only resurrected everything he tried so hard to bury.

Instead, he said, "Forget it, let's get it over and done with." He got out of the car and walked towards the entrance as though entering a den of lions. Slightly ahead, he missed the hurt expression on Alice's face.

It took a lot of restraint not to extricate his arm from hers as she caught up with him at the door. Inside, a few of the waiters greeted him in familiar tones. He noted the strange look the manager flashed him when he came over to receive them.

Ugo groaned inwardly. Everything reminded him of her. The food might have been tasty, but he didn't notice it. That Alice was in a chatty mood and did most of the talking was a relief. He did not trust himself to string two complete sentences together. Forcing his thoughts from straying to Uzo was stressing him out.

"Let's order dessert," Alice said, as the waiter cleared their plates away.

Ugo glanced at the exit "I am a little full and really have to get back to work."

"What's the use of dinner without dessert? We will just order ice cream."

Ugo gave what he hoped was a smile and let her make the order. Within minutes, the waiter returned with two crystal bowls that held a mixture of strawberry and vanilla flavored ice cream and a thin wafer stuck at the side. After thanking him, Alice asked him to wait. She "oohed" and "aahed" over the dessert, dug into her bag and brought out her phone.

"Could you take a picture of us?" The young man nodded, a smile creasing his lips. Ugo protested, but Alice insisted.

"Smile…" She bared beautiful set of teeth for the camera and, just as the flash was about to come on, he felt a weight on his shoulder. It lifted before he could react. She took back her phone and slipped it into her bag.

"I am not really a picture person. I hope it comes out all right."

"Hmm."

"Ugo what's going on? You are such a chatterbox when you are on Facebook Messenger, but this evening you have hardly spoken a word."

"I am sorry, Alice, I just have a lot of work on my mind. Are you done? Can we go now?"

"Maybe we can schedule a redo of this dinner in a month or thereabout?" she asked sweetly. Ugo raised his brow.

"Um, okay, whatever."

They headed out, his strides long beside Alice, who struggled in her heels to keep up. At the car, Ugo heard the precise voice he had hoped to avoid.

"My son, what a pleasure to see you again. Where is my daughter?"

Baba sat in his usual spot under the mango tree. He looked pointedly at Alice. His expression said it all. Ugo felt even smaller.

"Baba meet my friend Alice. Alice, this is Baba."

"Alice. What a pretty name for a pretty girl. God bless you." Alice shifted on her feet and slid behind Ugo.

"We have to go now, Baba. Take care."

"Bye, my son."

Ugo couldn't wait to get back to his house and bury his head in work. The whole evening had been a disaster. It brought back too many Uzo related thoughts to his mind, especially the way he had treated her after the information he received about her family. She didn't deserve that. He should have called and had a conversation instead of ghosting her the way he did. In his defense, he had been confused. One minute he was certain he had met the woman he wanted to spend the rest of his life with, the next he finds out she is a maniacal crazy woman with tendencies towards insanity. His knee-jerk reaction was to flee, and he knew it had been the cowardly thing to do. Now he had to fight the guilt, the shame, and the loss.

Chapter Nine

THE NEXT MORNING, ALICE gave Tope an update of the night before.

"It didn't go the way I thought it would. I had to keep the conversation going all through the entire evening. He was way different from the chatty, funny Ugo I exchanged banter with on Facebook. Almost like he didn't even want to be with me."

Tope brushed her comments away with a wave.

"Look, my sister, these are mere relationship birth pains. When the ice breaks, you guys will hit it off properly. Did you take the picture like I told you?"

"Yes, I did. I looked great in it, but he looked funny."

"Let me see." She took Alice's phone and zoomed in on the picture.

"Not too bad. You are glowing. I love the head on shoulder move." She winked at Alice. "He just looked serious. Luckily, it was not a frown. Now post it on Facebook and stake your claim."

"How will I do that?" Alice's forehead creased.

"What do you think the tag function is there for? You tag him, tag everybody you know, and put one solid caption that says nothing, but really says everything."

"I'm confused. Why am I tagging him?"

Tope shook her head.

"So, he sees what is possible. He might not be thinking about it. Sometimes you have to help people by giving them a little nudge. When he sees the picture and how good you guys look, it will all come together."

Alice nodded, understanding dawning.

"And don't forget to tag Uzo."

"Why? She is hardly on Facebook, and isn't that mean? Like rubbing salt on a wound."

"Yes. Do you have any idea what happens to such a wound? After the initial hurt, the salt disinfects the injury and speeds up the healing process."

Alice looked doubtful.

"Okay, wait. She said she's moving on, right? Ehen, she has moved on; you have moved in. *Nothing spoil.*"

Alice imagined the hurt she would cause her friend. It really did not give her pleasure.

"Alice, this is not the time to back down," she insisted when Alice turned slightly away from her. "You have a mission. Focus on the endgame. We need to ensure Uzo is totally out of the picture so Ugo can focus on you." She grabbed Alice's shoulder and turned her around to face her. "Wipe that frown off your face. You need this, girl. Imagine wedding bells and your happy marriage."

Alice nodded. She wrote a caption, tagged as many people as she could including Uzo and, squashing the last vestige of guilt, clicked send. In an instant, the picture uploaded on social media.

"Done."

Tope accessed Facebook from her phone and checked her notifications. She grinned broadly, reading what Alice had written aloud,

'Night out with a very special friend.' She laughed at the wink emoji.

Tope high-fived her friend and quickly added a comment in the comment section under the post, 'Are congratulations in order?' She added three wink emojis, and tagged a few of her own friends, including some of her media contacts.

"Now, let all the magic happen." She grinned at Alice.

UZO HAD PROMISED HERSELF she would delete the Facebook app from her phone, but she still hadn't and occasionally, even though she knew she shouldn't, she logged in to see what Ugo was up to.

She logged in that Monday evening and her heart sunk all the way to her feet when she saw the picture of her best friend, looking so beautiful with Ugo, her... her thoughts halted. He was her nothing, but still. A very special friend? When did that happen? She wrapped a hand around her throat, swallowing hard. A throbbing headache erupted, threatening to split her skull. Why were people congratulating her? She called Alice to find out what was really going on. Once she picked the call, Uzo cut right to the chase.

"Hey, Alice, how are you? I was just on Facebook. What's up with you and Ugo and being special friends?"

Uzo heard her cough and rummage through something, she was not sure. There was a lot of static, then silence. She thought the call had dropped, then her voice came through loud and clear.

"Honestly, I was surprised at the invitation to dinner. I just went with the flow. I hope it's okay with you. I said, let me explore."

"Explore? With him? When you know how I feel… sorry… knowing I felt about him?"

"I don't like the way you are making it sound. Anybody listening will think I stole your man or something. I don't appreciate that at all."

Uzo sighed. She slowly sat down in her dinning chair and rested her head on her palm. It was not fair to blame Alice. The feeling of rejection she still carried from her last two failed relationships was playing havoc with her emotions.

"Don't mind me, jare, I am just oversensitive right now. God is in control. That's why Ugo didn't respond to me after I left Lagos. He may have used me to get to you. You know, it won't be the first time." Her train of thought made her restless. She rose and paced around her living room.

"Why are you bringing up the University again? Derin was an idiot. He shouldn't have hurt you that way."

"That's life, isn't it? You will always be the beautiful princess, and I, the ugly stepsister."

"Don't you ever say that again. There is a man out there, who will see you for the beauty that you are."

"Yeah, I thought that was Ugo, but apparently it was all just words. I hope it works out for you and he shows you his own true colors. I never want you to hurt the way I am."

"He can never try that. My eyes are wide open."

UZO FELT THE BARB but did not respond to it. "Do you mind though, while the idea of both of you sinks in, please, don't tag me in your photos together. I'm not jealous or anything. It's just that the hurt is still there. After a few months I'll be able to handle it, but trust me, I will always be happy for you. You are my best friend. Let us talk later."

After the call, Uzo closed her eyes and took deep breaths, murmuring words of affirmation to herself. "Uzo, you are strong, you will be okay. It's just like the last time, you will survive this." Her mind heard the words and understood it, but her heart did not.

ALICE HELD THE PHONE to her ear long after her friend hung up.

Chapter Ten

ALICE LONG EXPECTED THE call, but not his reaction.

"What exactly did you think you were doing?" He boomed above the loud background noise.

"What do you mean?"

"You know what I mean. The picture you posted on Facebook, and what kind of caption was that?"

Alice lazily picked up her box of office pins, spilled them on her desk and started arranging them haphazardly.

"Ugo calm down. I am not sure why you are getting so worked up."

"I am worked up!"

Alice took the phone off her ear and stared at it like it was a foreign object. This guy was really yelling at her. She could not believe it. "What is your problem with the picture?"

"Do I have to spell it out to you? 'A special evening with a special someone'? How are we special?"

"Ugo, are we not friends? Everyone I call my friend is special to me." She smiled at her handy work. She had completed a perfect heart.

"I don't understand your definition of special, Alice, but the blog that picked up that picture has assumed all sorts."

It thrilled Alice that a blog carried the story. Tope was definitely a genius. She couldn't wait to check it out.

"I can't be responsible for what other people think, can I?" she asked with all the indifference she could muster.

"Do you know what? I agree with you there, forget all the others. Why in heaven's name did you tag Uzo? What kind of message were you trying to send?"

"I think the problem here is you. You are reading too much into everything." She started on her second heart shape. "Uzo is my best friend. Why would I not tag her if I went out with a mutual friend?"

"Alice, I don't know what your game is, but I don't like it. I don't like being used or being taken for a fool, and that is what I feel you are doing to me right now. I would appreciate it if you took down that post."

"Ugo, I will not take it down. It is my picture. It is my Facebook feed." Her tone tightened. Taking orders was not something she did well.

"Take that post down, now," he barked.

She ruffled the hearts across the table with a wave of her hand, and rose, her face contorted in anger.

"Don't you ever raise your voice at me, Ugo Nwokedi. I am not Uzo!"

A few seconds of silence settled, and she could hear his heavy breathing, then he said, "No, you are definitely not her."

"I FEEL LIKE A fool!" Ugo balled his fist and thumped his palm, pacing his room. It had been a long time since Ugo had been this upset with anybody, and Alice's feigned innocence upset him even more.

The posted picture he could absorb. Lately, people post every aspect of their lives on social media, but something about tagging Uzo did not sit right. It was a mean thing to do and cast aspersions on everything he thought about Alice, which was not much, but it made him doubt what she had told him about Uzo. What if none of it was true? What if Uzo was not some undercover mad person?

The thought sent him reeling. Why had he taken Alice's word completely, without even talking to Uzo about it? He thought back to how he treated her, and guilt flowed afresh. It had been a month since that weekend, but he could not get her out of his mind. He constantly missed her. She was the first person he wanted to call about work, about stuff that happened to him during the day. He wanted to hear her laugh at his jokes. He also wanted to be there for her in case she needed somebody to talk to. His insides were in a turmoil. He had tried praying about it but had no peace so far.

"Father God, I am so sorry. I know the root of this matter is my fear of witchcraft and demonic activities due to the sort of the family I grew up in. But you have not given me a spirit of fear, but of power, love, and a sound mind."

Resolutely, he picked up his phone and dialed Uzo's number. "God," he whispered under his breath. "Please, let her pick up."

The phone rang. He dialed repeatedly. It was not unusual. She might be busy. He tried again after work, around 8 p.m. It was usually around this time they would have their conversations till late into the night. It rang out. He sent a SMS. "Uzo, I need to speak with you."

He called after a few minutes. Ugo kept this up for an entire week, leaving countless voice and text messages. Eventually, the lines stopped ringing, and the messages were not delivered.

"This lady has blocked me," he concluded one afternoon. The thought that he would never speak to her again brought to the fore the hold she held over his heart. He had thrown away something precious. Misery overwhelmed him and it showed in his work.

WOLE AYOMIDE RAN THE poultry division of the Nwadike enterprise. He managed farms across the country. His job required constant travels, just like his boss and friend Ugo. The opportunities for both of them to be in the same state at the same time were rare and far between. So Wole was disappointed at the perpetual state of despondency in which Ugo languished these days. He had hoped it would pass, but this was the second week running since his arrival and Wole felt it was time he said something, especially after catching him intermittently staring at his phone and then into space.

"Ugo, is your distraction because of the same lady?"

Ugo gave a vague story about a situation with a friend. He shook his phone in the air and said through gritted teeth, "The calls are not even going through anymore. The babe has blocked me on all communication channels."

"I wish you had allowed me to see this girl just once." He grinned, giving Ugo a wink.

"Wole, not now, please."

"Too soon? I get it. What I don't understand is, if you really like her, why did you cut her off in the first place?"

"Because I am a fool, that's why." He hung his head low.

Wole stared at his friend in surprise. He had heard that when some men fall in love, they fall hard. He had never seen Ugo in this state before. He was the guy who never had a shortage of female admirers, not only because of his successful career but also his personality. He was the quintessential charmer. He made ladies laugh and feel at ease, but if they ever wanted anything more, he slid away and "friend zoned" himself. So, the ladies stayed his friends, gave up any romantic notions, and married other people. Not once had he regretted a potential relationship growing cold. He absolutely enjoyed the life of a bachelor.

Ugo's eyes lit up. "Wole, you have to help me. You know, normally I won't involve you in my personal affairs like this. Can you call her?"

Wole stepped back, and his forehead creased. "Call her and say what?"

"Just call her. Let her pick the call and I'll take it from there."

"Hmm, Okay. Like you said, it's very unlike you. This obviously is a serious situation." He went to his desk and got his phone. "Oya, call out the number to me."

He dialed and waited. Wole wished he could take a picture of Ugo's face so he could tease him later. Now, he was desperately chewing his lower lip and looking at Wole like he had the answers to the meaning of life.

The ticking seconds as the phone rang felt like hours to Wole. He could not imagine how Ugo felt. A voice came on suddenly and relief washed over him. He cleared his throat and said, "Hold on for your caller, Ma'am."

Before he could hand the phone over, Ugo grabbed it. He did not speak at once. He took deep breaths, moving the cellphone from one hand to the other.

Finally, eyes closed, he said, "Hey, Uzo… hey, please, don't hang up. I beg you… I am so sorry. I was desperate… you have blocked me everywhere… I didn't know what to do… I know it's work time; can I call you tonight? … Okay, tomorrow? … Give me a time, whatever works for you."

He ran his hand over his head and left it there, listening intently.

"I'll take it… Friday 9 p.m... Wait, you'll have to unblock my line… Thank you so much. Uzo… I am sorry."

He sat down and buried his face in his hand, the phone clutched to his chest.

"Erm, guy, my phone."

"Oh," he opened his eyes and returned the phone, "I'm sorry."

"That was intense. What did you say you did again?"

"Let me sort this issue out. I promise to bring you up to speed." Weariness seeped into his body, after all the adrenalin. He moved to the settee in his office and lay down.

"No problem. But if you are this pent up today, how will you manage till Friday?"

Ugo had no idea.

Chapter Eleven

THE WEEK WAS TORTUROUS for both Uzo and Ugo. Ugo practiced what he would say over and over, but none of his speeches worked in his mind. He panicked at the possibility that she would never forgive him.

Uzo regretted moving the call so far away, but she wasn't ready to hear him explain his relationship with Alice. Maybe he wanted to tell her himself that they were now a couple. The pain she felt just imagining it was intense. She did not need the confirmation just yet, and the extra the time would give her emotions a bit of room to breathe but it was a wasted effort. The minute she heard his voice that Friday evening, all her emotions came sweeping through her entire system and she blurted out.

"What was that behavior about?"

"Uzo, I..."

A part of her cautioned herself to keep things under control, but she could not. She had cried too many tears for him, not knowing what was going on. Now she needed answers.

"I thought we had something good; the beginning of something special and you treated me like I was nothing! All you had to do was tell me the truth. You wanted us to be friends, but your real interest was in Alice. Why make me travel across the country for that?"

"Woah! whoa! Uzo, wait…. How did Alice *enter our matter?* The planned weekend was for both of us. I am not interested, and I have never been interested, and will NEVER be interested in Alice."

"Please, don't play games with me. You asked her out to dinner, you guys took a picture, posted it on Facebook and then tagged me!"

"Uzo, let…"

"No, Ugo, you wanted this call, let me say my piece. You have hurt me deeply. Why did you have to go so far? The way you spoke, the things you said, the Baba episode....why did you make me fall... forget it. I shouldn't blame you. You simply played your game too well."

Uzo finally could not hold it and burst into tears. Ugo's heart shattered into a million pieces at her words, and when she broke down, his eyes brimmed over as well. He should not have had this conversation away from her. He should have been there to hold her if she would let him. This episode added a layer to his guilt. He did not handle this properly.

"Uzo... please, stop crying, please." His voice trembled. "Uzo, are you listening? Please, let me explain. I hurt you by disappearing, and for that I am so sorry, but this Alice story is far from true. I did not ask her out, she asked me out. I did not even want to go. The picture you saw, she took it, posted and tagged you. I had nothing to do with it, I swear it. And while we are talking about Alice..."

"Stop it, Ugo. Take responsibility for your actions too. No one forced you to do any of those things. Do you also blame Alice for how you treated me before you guys hooked up?"

He wished he could go through the phone and shake it into her head that there was no Alice in the picture. Even the thought made his skin crawl. Maybe that was what Alice wanted to achieve by all this. He had no clue how to unravel himself out of this web she had created.

"Uzo, you are right. I take responsibility but, please, hear me out on Alice. The Monday you left, she told me some things that honestly frightened me and instead of talking it over with you, I did the cowardly and irresponsible thing. I ran. I am so ashamed of myself, but I did."

"What are you talking about? What did you hear from Alice?"

"She told me…" Now that he was about to repeat it, he felt foolish. "She told me that insanity runs in your family… and you have traces of it, that in high school you almost killed a fellow pupil when you cracked his skull in anger. Everyone knew you then as the crazy girl with a crazy father. She also insinuated that it was hereditary. I am so sorry I believed her. I know this sounds silly… please…"

"Ugo, I'll call you back. I have to talk to Alice about this. It won't be right to think what I am thinking without clearing with her first."

Panic seized him. "Do you promise you'll call me?"

"I promise." Her voice was barely a whisper.

Ugo paced his room for twenty minutes, his hand itching to call her, wondering if Alice was making up more stories. He also felt ashamed that Uzo showed a million times more integrity than he had done. She was doing what he should have done when he heard the story from Alice. He should have called her right away. He wouldn't be in this mess. Just when he was ready to throw off restraint and dial her number, his phone beeped.

"Uzo."

"Yeah… it took a little longer than I thought. She said she told you those things. What I had a problem establishing was the why."

Ugo noticed that her tone was now cool and drained of emotion. It scared him.

"I assure you I do not believe a single word…"

"Oh, but you should. Everything she said was true."

"Really?" Ugo sat heavily in his chair. He felt air was being sucked out of him.

"Yes, really Ugo, but she didn't finish the entire story. I broke a cement block on the social prefect's head way back in Senior Secondary. He had dragged me behind an uncompleted building and tried to rape me. I fought like a wild animal. I don't know how my knee contacted his groin but soon he curled up in pain. Yes, I was furious, I grabbed the nearest block and smashed it on his head. I hit as hard as I could and ran to the House Mistress, who took both of us to a hospital. He suffered a fractured skull that eventually healed, and lost interest in girls after that. But isn't it funny how no one remembered the attempted rape? Yet they all remembered the angry girl."

Ugo cradled his head, his body rocking back on forth. What had he done? Her voice came through his speakers.

"So that's it for the first accusation. As for the second, my father being insane…"

Ugo felt the reprimand. He deserved it. He did not know how adequately to apologize. She remained silent. He could hear her taking deep breaths and exhaling. Finally, she spoke.

"I do not think you deserve to know this, but because I am uncomfortable with the idea of my father's image being tarnished, I will tell you. My father married my mother in his 50's. I was their only child. By the time I was 15, he was 65. We noticed short-lived moments when he couldn't remember his name. Those episodes grew longer and sometimes he didn't know us either. Many times, he ended up on the streets confused and someone would bring him home. Then one day as my father ran out of the house in pure terror, he ran into a moving traffic and got hit by a car."

"Oh, no, Uzo! I am so sorry." He wished again he had had this conversation in person. "I am no doctor, but it sounds like he may have had Alzheimer's Disease."

"Thank you for that. Now that I know more, I think so, too. But then, he just seemed crazy, especially when on the street looking for his childhood home and none of us knew what he meant. Children were not kind and threw stones at him. He slept outside under the open skies, refusing to follow my mother in. He did not know who she was. It took days before he remembered us again."

Ugo slid off the chair to the floor, regret washing over him in a continuous wave. If only he had made that call to her first.

"Uzo, I should not have jumped to conclusions. Please, forgive me." He heard her give a dry laugh.

"I forgive you, Ugo. You do not owe me anything. We were just friends, remember?"

"I do not want to be just friends. That weekend was special for me as it was for you. I was already building a future."

"Hmm, then you hear something about me and the first thing you do is believe the worst and treat me like a piece of trash. You didn't even have the decency, Ugo, to find out if I made it back to Abuja safely. I have been hurt too many times in my life.

I will not put myself in the hands of a person like you, I don't feel safe with you."

"Uzo, please." His voice came out hoarse.

"Thank you, Ugo. I wish you all the best in life."

UZO CUT THE CALL and curled up in a ball beside her bed. She tightened her arms around her stomach and allowed the self-control she had on as an armor to shatter. She screamed, feeling herself drowning, and fast. She could not handle this. The two people who meant the most to her had cut her heart into pieces. It was unbearable. She felt herself losing her mind.

How could Alice hate her so much to do something like this? A friend who stuck closer than a brother all these years. She was so sure Ugo lied about everything. When she called Alice, she had called to report him, but

Alice's uncharacteristic silence was telling.

"Alice, you were my best friend. How could you do this to me?" Then there was Ugo for whom she had built a home in her heart. The hurt was overwhelming. She struggled to gain charge of her emotions, but this was a battle she could not win.

"God, nooooo! This is too much for me!" she wailed into the dark room and sobbed till sleep took over.

Chapter Twelve

UGO HAD A TERRIBLE weekend. He hardly ate or slept. He tried repeatedly to reach Uzo to no avail He took solace in the fact that she hadn't blocked him again.

"Ha! My guy, what happened to you? Are you sick?" Wole asked on walking into the office on Monday morning.

"I'm good. Don't worry."

"I don't know what mirror you are using, but you look terrible."

Ugo sat at his desk and opened his laptop.

"How did your call go?" Wole, who sat across from him, noticed Ugo wince at the question. "Not too good, I presume. I am sorry, bro."

He reached over and rubbed his friend's shoulder. Ugo slammed the laptop shut, pushed it away and bent over. He rested his head in the crook of his arm. Wole's heart went out to him.

"Have you prayed about this?"

"I have, I think. I don't even know anymore," he said, his voice muffled due to the way he sat.

"Since that isn't an answer, do you mind if I do so now?"

Ugo nodded; head still bent. Wole closed his eyes and lifted his hands skyward. "Father, you know and see all things. I commit my friend and this relationship to you. If this is your will, I ask for your wisdom, that you guide him in making the right decision and I pray for this girl, whoever she is. Father, be with her and grant her peace concerning your will for her, in Jesus name."

"Amen," Ugo intoned. "Thanks so much, Wole."

By evening, he was still mulling over Wole's plea for wisdom and he echoed the prayer.

"Father, you know all things. Give me something, give me an idea that will soften her heart. If you do this for me, I promise to honor the treasure your daughter is. I won't hurt her like this again. In Jesus' Name. I also resist the spirit of fear, Almighty God. I refuse to be bound anymore."

That night, he slept well for the first time since this debacle. The next morning, he awoke with the first picture of Baba in his head, the old man at the Cafe.

"Father God, what are you telling me?" He received no response. Still burning with curiosity, he bathed, dressed up and rushed to the Love Legacy café. He scanned the parking lot, searching for him with no luck. He entered the restaurant wondering if anybody would be there at 9 a.m. and saw a man mopping the floor.

"Good morning, my brother."

The man paused in his cleaning. "Good morning, Sir, *we never open o, na* till 12."

"I'm not here to buy food. Please. Where is the old man who sits outside at the park?"

"Oh, Baba? *We never see am for some time o. In fact, na even just yesterday we bin dey talk am. Where Baba dey?*"

"Okay, those times he comes around, what time does he usually get here?"

The man scratched his head, his face contorted in deep thought. *"If say e won come. Maybe around dat kain six o'clock for evening."*

"Okay, thank you." Ugo raised a fist in greeting on his way out. "Thank you so much. I'll be back by six."

"Oga shey no wahala shaa?"

"No problem at all."

Ugo kept checking the time till the clock struck five. He entered his car and drove straight to Lekki. The traffic delayed him, and he got to the café around 6.30 p.m. By this time, the restaurant was at full capacity, business was obviously booming. The car park was full. He searched in-between cars for Baba, unable to find him, he went around the back and sighted the guy he had spoken to earlier.

"Hey, Oga, na you?" He waved to Ugo, who waved back. *"Baba never come o. You go try tomorrow?"*

Ugo left disappointed. It worsened as he tried his luck the next two days without success. He collected the cleaner's name and number and left him instructions to call him once he sighted Baba or had any information about him.

He never stopped praying or calling Uzo. His efforts did not yield visible results until he got a call from Lewis, the cleaner, on the fourth day. His heart quickened. He almost wept when he heard the words that Baba was back. He packed up his stuff and shuttled to Lekki once again. He had driven along this axis in the past week more times than he had in an entire year.

He saw Baba seated under a tree, looking slightly stressed, and ran up to him. He was just finishing his dinner. Ugo prostrated on the floor before joining him on the bench.

"Baba. What happened to you?"

His greeting elicited a warm smile from the old man once he recognized him. "My son, how are you?" He lowered his bowl to the ground and turned to face Ugo.

"I'm fine, Baba. I have been looking everywhere for you."

"You are looking for me? *I hope no problem.*"

"No, Baba, but where have you been? You do not look too good."

Baba shook his head slowly. He brought out some sachets of tablets from a pouch beside him and showed Ugo. "My son. I had a terrible bout of malaria. I almost thought it was time for me to go, but God said not yet."

"I'm so sorry to hear that. I'm so glad you're better."

"We give God praise." He carefully ejected two round white tablets and two smaller white ones. He held the pills in his palm. "Why have you been looking for me?"

"Baba, I need your help." Ugo picked up the bottle of water beside him and handed it over to Baba. The old man took a mouthful and swirled it around his mouth before swallowing. He took another gulp, this time he added the tablets and swallowed it all. Baba squeezed his eyes shut as the liquid made its way down his throat. "Aaah." He dropped the bottle beside him, bent forward and entwined his hands around his knees. He turned to Ugo.

"What can I do to help? Tell me, you are such a kind boy and I have missed seeing you and my daughter, the first one, not the second one." He winked.

Ugo smiled. "Yes, Baba. That's the reason I'm here."

"I hope she's all right."

"She's all right, but we are not all right."

"Hm." He nodded knowingly. "So, what did you do to my girl?"

"Baba. I'm too ashamed to say, but somehow, I feel that you are part of my solution towards getting her back."

"Really?" He turned fully to face Ugo.

"She really likes you. I want you to help me beg her. What I did was wrong, and she is right to be angry, but she won't give me a chance to make amends. God knows I am terribly sorry."

Baba leaned back against the nearby tree and closed his eyes. Ugo waited patiently, rubbing his hands together.

"My son, that lady is special. You cannot treat an egg the way you do a rock. Do you promise you would be kind and considerate, and not treat her *anyhow* again?"

Ugo returned to his prostate position.

"I promise you," he responded solemnly.

"Okay, get up. What do you need me to do?"

"Thank you, Sir. I want you to talk to her through a video recording I will send to her. I know that if she sees you, she will listen."

"I have never done a video call before. You will have to teach me."

"It's easy, Baba. Just speak and I will do the recording."

For the next few minutes, Baba did as he promised. When he finished, Ugo had tears in his eyes. He reached for his wallet, but Baba stopped him.

"Not this time. What I want is to see both of you together again, then we will celebrate. You can bring me a bottle of wine then."

"Amen, Sir. Thank you and keep well."

Ugo hurried back to his car. He had a lot of arrangements to make.

Chapter Thirteen

"BUZZ, BUZZ," UZO GLANCED at the vibrating phone on her table but did not check it. She wondered if it was Ugo, and then chided herself for the thought. She was the one who prayed he would stop his incessant calls and when he stopped, she struggled with that too. It had been two days, and since then she reached for her phone often to check if he called.

The WhatsApp message was from an unknown number, and only a video. She hated forwards and was tempted to ignore it, but curiosity got the better of her.

She pressed play, expecting everything else but what came through. Baba's wrinkled face garnished with an enormous smile and his firm voice came through the speakers, just like she remembered him from not so long ago, her eyes filled with tears as she listened to him speak.

"My daughter, how are you?" He waved into the camera. "I have missed you but hope to see you again soon." He cleared his throat. "My son told me he has done something he is ashamed of and seeks your forgiveness. To err is human but forgiveness is divine. You, my daughter, have a touch of divine in you. I know it. I am not here to say you must forgive. I only beg that you give him a chance to, hopefully, mend fences. Would you do this for me, my child? I hope you will consider. God loves you and so do I."

The video ended and his withered face disappeared from the screen. The tears flowed. While she contemplated, her phone rang again. She identified the caller and picked at once.

"Why did you drag that poor old man into this?" She tried to keep the sternness in her voice but could not.

She heard him say, "I had no choice, and I felt God led me to do it. I didn't know what else to do.

Please, give me a chance. Let's just talk."

"Give me an hour or two. I am still at work."

"Take all the time you need. I'll sit here till you are done."

Uzo rose from behind her desk cocking her head to the side. "Wait, what does that mean? You'll sit here, sit where?"

"I am at the reception room in your office."

The sound of her heart thumping filled her ears, and she felt a sudden rush of blood to her head. She sat back heavily.

"What, you are in Abuja?"

"Yes, Uzo, and with good reason. We really need to see each other."

She dialed her secretary with shaky hands.

"Tosin, is there anybody at the reception for me? … describe him…" Uzo's heart pounded so hard, she thought it would explode. Ugo was here! "Okay. Send him up in five minutes."

Uzo dashed to her bathroom. She checked her face, added a fresh coat of lip gloss and loosened her braids from the bun she had put up this morning. She let her hair fall across her shoulders, added a spritz of perfume behind both cars and took a deep breath. She eyed herself one last time.

She walked back to her desk and called Tosin to let him in. She came around and sat on the table edge, folded her hands and waited for him to enter.

"Don't lose your head, Uzo. You are a mature woman, not a child. Stop being so jittery and remember, he still betrayed you."

Her heart betrayed her the instant Ugo walked in with an enormous bouquet of red roses, looking hesitant. Something let loose inside her. She forgot her pep talk and raced into his arms. Ugo lifted her off the ground the minute she got to him. A stunned looked on his face.

"Oh God, thank you," he breathed into her neck. He twirled her around before dropping her slowly, refusing to let her go. He held her tightly just in case he was dreaming, the roses forgotten and crushed beneath their feet.

"Uzo, I am so sorry I hurt you. I was wrong. Please, forgive me."

He reluctantly pulled away and cupped her face in his hands, wiping the streaks of tears that ran down her cheeks with his thumbs.

"I missed you so much, my Uzo. Having you out of my life was the worst experience I have ever had. I really thought I would die. There is no other way to put it. I love you; I love you so much."

Uzo felt her legs tremble. She was certain this was all a dream. He led her to the office couch and made her sit. He pulled her into his arms so that her head rested on his shoulder as she whimpered.

"Uzo, please, what do you need me to do so we can move past this? I will do anything."

"I don't know. I am scared. What if I open my heart again and you change your mind tomorrow? We really don't know each other well. It's as if we skipped friendship to something else without even realizing it."

"Then let's do friends. If that's what you want."

"But how can we be just friends? You just told me you loved me?"

"Ehen? Can't I love my friend?" Ugo said and Uzo gave a watery smile.

"I'll be your friend for as long as you need me to be, but I know what I want." His movements made her sit up, and she saw him dip his hand in his pocket and bring out a black box. Uzo moved away from him, her mouth open and her eyes wide.

"What's that?"

"You know what it is," he whispered. Something in his eyes sent a shiver through her body. He flipped the box open. Inside was the most beautiful 18ct white gold engagement ring with three round brilliant cut diamonds nestled in a base of black velvet. Uzo blinked in confusion. Sensing her emotions, he said with a smile, "Fear not, I'm not asking you to marry me now, but I want you to know, Uzo Madumere, that this is where I want to end up. I'm not playing games with you. I want us to know each other so that a day like this will come when I'll slip this ring on your finger."

The genuineness of his words calmed her, but only a little. What if he was saying all the right words again? "Ugo, you really, really hurt me."

Her words pierced his soul like a dagger. "I know, and I pledge to spend the rest of my life making it up to you by God's grace. Even if we're only friends, I will never hurt you like that again." His hands kept up a steady rhythm as he stroked her braids, running his fingers from her head to her shoulders. "Please, give us a chance, Uzo. Get to know me better. I will wait for as long as it takes for you to arrive at a place you can trust me again."

"What happens when I get there?"

"To that place of trust? You jab me on my side and that's my cue to get down on one knee. But only when you know for sure you can trust me. Will that work for you?"

She nodded into his chest, all the sadness and anxiety of the past month lifting. She played with his shirt buttons, still needing more evidence that this was not a dream.

"I can't believe you are here. When do you go back?"

"I cleared up my schedule for the whole week."

"A whole week?" She sat up to look at him, stunned. She knew the tight work schedule he kept. He was three times busier than she was. The enormity of his gesture was not lost. Her eyes went misty again.

"Why do you think it took me so long to get here? I didn't know how long it would take to get you back. I wasn't taking chances, but if I had known that once I came, you would gel so easily," he rubbed her chin between his thumb and forefingers," I would have booked my flight for this afternoon."

She punched him at his side. "I pitied you. It's all thanks to Baba you are even in this office."

"*Abegii*, you couldn't resist my charms, Baba or no Baba."

She sat up and pointed to the door. "*Oya, leave my office. I no do again.*"

"*Ah ahn*, madam," laughing, he pulled her back to his side, "okay, you did not run into my arms when I walked in. I was the one who ran into yours, and you carried me around."

"Ugo!" She pushed herself away from him, farther this time. He raised both hands in mock surrender.

"You know what? You write the memory, I will remember whatever you want me to. I don't want *wahala*."

She settled back in his arms, grinning from ear to ear. He adjusted her so her head lay on his chest. He relished the feel of her in his arms and would have promised her half his kingdom if she wanted it.

"Thank you for coming."

"I wouldn't want to be anywhere else."

Chapter Fourteen

THE WEEK FLEW BY for both lovebirds. Ugo was at her office promptly each morning at 7:30 a.m. He introduced himself to all the staff as her new Personal Assistant and did the work so well that her actual personal assistant called for a meeting to enquire if her job was still safe.

Ugo saw her at work, both on the farm and in her office. He attended and sat in on all her meetings. He stayed in the background and carried her bag and files so no one recognized him as Ugo Nwokedi. He enjoyed the anonymity.

After work, they strolled around or sat on the park benches within Uzo's residential estate till late at night. He booked a room at a bed-and-breakfast nearby, and this afforded him the luxury of more time with her. They made friends with the security guards, who patrolled the estate at night. Despite the long hours spent in each other's company, saying goodbye every night was getting harder.

On Sunday evening, they had a last dinner at a small fancy restaurant in town. Ugo was booked for the first flight back to Lagos the next day. The atmosphere was somber. Both lovers were reluctant to end the evening, so when Ugo suggested a walk, Uzo jumped at it. He dropped her off at the park entrance and drove on to park the car outside her apartment, less than a minute away.

While she waited, Uzo dwelt on the sad reminder that it was their last night together. She had no idea how she would handle him being gone and choked back the tears again. She did not want Ugo's memories of their last night together to be of him consoling her. She tried to pull herself together just as one of the night guards, Samuel, the youngest of the security team, passed her.

"*Madam, na you?*"

"Yes, Samuel. How are you today?" She smiled. She liked Samuel.

"*I dey o. Madam, I see Oga for road, e come tell me say e dey go Lagos tomorrow.*"

"Yes, he leaves first thing in the morning." A feeling of intense loss washed over her.

"*Chaii, we think say Oga dey here for Abuja and maybe soon, una go … you know.*" He gave a cheeky grin.

The couple unknowingly provided entertainment for the night security patrol. They had placed bets on how soon a wedding would be. They all loved Madam Uzo as they called her. She was one of the nicer residents of the estate and they were rooting for her.

"No, Samuel, we are just… we are just…" The word stuck in her throat. She knew it was not true. They were way more than friends. She did not want the tag of 'just friends' anymore but Ugo had said he would go at her own pace, so if there would be a change in their status, she had to do something about it.

"Madam?"

"Mmm, what Samuel?" She had forgotten he was there.

"*No, you dey talk sometin, next tin you just stop.*"

"I'm sorry, Samuel."

"*No wahala, Ma, I don see Oga dey come.*"

Uzo turned around and saw him jogging down. Her heart leaped at the sight of his silhouette and joy spread through her. She met him half-way and hugged him. Ugo, always down for a hug, responded as enthusiastically but could not help teasing.

"I was gone for just five minutes, lady. You are hugging me like I traveled out of the state."

Uzo held him tighter and sniffed his shirt, too overwhelmed to send a jibe back. He noticed her mood and sobered up.

"Hey, babe, just so you know, I'm only cracking jokes to stop myself from joining in your tears. I am howling on the inside. Like the terrible kind, with snot and all. It's not a pretty sight." Without looking, he knew she was smiling. He felt her shiver and rubbed the side of her arms to ward off some of the chill, then led her to the bench she had just vacated. He pointed into the darkness where the silhouettes of two men in uniform could be seen behind a tree. They were probably smoking. Ugo and Uzo had seen them at it once or twice.

"Something tells me two wailing adults are not prime entertainment for the security team." He draped his arms across the back of the bench and stretched a bit.

"We have talked about this." He continued as a matter of fact. "We will be in touch every day. I'll be back in two weeks for the weekend, and the week after that you'll come over to Lagos. We can do this. No more tears, okay?" When she did not respond, he leaned over and pecked her softly on both cheeks. The jab at his side was unexpected.

"Ouch! Why did you do that?" He sat back, rubbing his side. "Uzo, I may have to report you for domestic violence. But if we are outdoors, is it still domestic? Hmm, we should discuss this…."

"Ugo, I am jabbing you!" And she did it one more time, glaring at him pointedly.

He stared at her like she had grown horns. She was trying to say something, but he did not know what it was.

"Ugh!" Uzo rose from the bench and stomped away a few paces until Ugo called out to her. She turned to find him on one knee. In a heartbeat, she ran back to him. He held out his hand, and she placed her left hand in his. Her entire body trembled in anticipation. It was impossible to keep her emotions at bay. He fumbled with one hand to get the box out of his pocket, succeeded and flipped it open to reveal a rock that glimmered in the moonlight.

"Uzo, sometimes I am really slow, please, bear with me. The Holy Spirit helped to me realize what you meant and saved my life." He bowed his head for a second. When he raised it, Uzo noticed the extra sheen in his eyes.

"I have been carrying this box around just hoping…Uzo Angela Madumere, I feel like I wasn't living before I met you. You came and changed my world. Wherever you are is where I want to be. To love you, to cherish you all my days. Will you do me the honor of being my wife?"

She knelt and held him. She did not want to let go. She never thought she could feel this way about anyone or that anyone would feel this way about her. Every other guy she had met always made her feel they were doing her a favor by being in relationship with her. Now here was a man, who thought marrying her was an honor. She was so grateful she had waited for him and not rushed or succumbed to the societal pressure to marry quickly.

"Yes, Ugo! A million times yes!" she wept for joy as he rose and engulfed her in another bear hug, lifting her off her feet.

"Thank you, Jesus!" he yelled into the night.

"Shh, it's late and people are sleeping," she chided laughing, excitement wrapping her insides. She wanted to scream and dance as well. To let the entire world know she said yes to the man who captured her heart.

"I am sorry but not sorry," he said in a loud whisper. "You have made me so happy! Come, let me take a picture. I need to capture this for posterity." He pulled her towards the nearest streetlamp and lifted her hands, so the light hit the ring, and took a picture of their hands entwined.

"Father, we thank you" He shook his head, instantly typing away on his phone.

"What are you doing?" She tried to see his phone screen but was not really interested. She was gazed at the ring on her finger, smiling so hard it felt like her face would split in half.

"I'm posting it on Facebook before you change your mind."

"You are so silly. Why would I change my mind?"

"Just making sure." He pulled her to his side and continued typing with his right hand.

"Really, what exactly are you doing?"

"I want to post this picture. Put a proper caption and tag the world, especially some people."

Her eyes widened in horror when she realized what he meant to do.

"Don't, Ugo." She tried to grab his phone. He swayed, side-stepping her reach.

"Why not?"

"Because it's petty, that's why." She could not get around him either. She stopped struggling and folded her arms, glaring as he typed away, giggling at the same time.

"Why can't you be the bigger man?" She huffed.

"Because I am not." He stuck his tongue out at her. "Done!" he cried joyfully. Hands in the air, he did a mini victory lap around her.

"You should be ashamed."

He came back to her and lowered his arms to pull her close.

"I am very ashamed, my soon- to- be Mrs. Nwokedi." He rubbed his nose against hers. Her body tingled, and for a minute none spoke. Ugo broke the contact and shook himself like a puppy, enjoying hearing Uzo laugh. He grabbed her hands and they continued walking.

"So, when are we doing this?" Ugo asked, swinging her hands back and forth. He stopped to look at the ring on her finger.

"I am thinking maybe a year from now?"

He stopped in his tracks and bent over laughing. 'A year? I'm sorry, that does not work for me. Something tells me it would not work for you either. Look at you, I am leaving for two weeks and you acted like I am off to war. I suggest we scrap that one-year idea right now and be more realistic. I prophesy that within six months, we will be in our house with you as Mrs. Ugo Nwokedi! The name is music to my ears."

"Six months?" Uzo bit her lip, contemplating the idea. "You don't think we are rushing into this, do you?"

He saw her worried expression and sobered quickly.

"I am ready to go to the registry tomorrow morning and make you my wife. I have never been more convinced about anything in my life. If you need more time, like I said earlier, that's okay too."

She reached out to him for a hug and whispered into his chest, "Thank you, Ugo for being so patient with me."

He gently rocked her and then said with mischief laced over his words, "Don't thank me with words. I want all gratitude paid in kind on our wedding night."

She giggled. Warmth spread through her body. She could not believe this was really happening. She did not think her heart could take any more happiness.

THE NEXT MORNING SOCIAL media was abuzz with the news of Ugo Nwokedi's engagement to a mystery woman. All that they had to go on was a picture of two entwined hands showing off a ring with a caption, 'Praise God, she said yes. Watch this space'. The first person he tagged was Alice.

Chapter Fifteen

ALICE HAD BEEN SICK for a while, but the doctors could not find anything physically wrong with her. At her last appointment, the doctor recommended she spoke with a therapist. The suggestion frightened her, but she knew the insomnia and lack of appetite was worsening.

She hated to admit that the illness started the day she saw the Facebook post about Ugo's engagement. She knew it was to Uzo. She recognized the birthmark on her hand with the dark patch on her fist, between her pinky and ring finger.

Nothing made sense after that. Her world turned grey with despair, and melancholy became her constant companion. She felt like she was constantly heading towards darkness and lately it was getting stronger. She knew that soon; she would be too weak to ward it off.

Her work suffered. Eventually, her boss placed her on a two-week medical leave. Afraid of being stuck at home alone, she begged to stay on at work, but management insisted she was now a liability and needed to sort herself out first. As head of Finance, her ability to focus was the line between a successful year and lawsuits with irate clients.

Alice feared the dark, not from outside, but within. She never wanted to be alone for long. The darkness grew heavier when she was alone. To avoid this, she started attending church again, where she heard God's word anew. The Holy Spirit worked on her, but she struggled, rationalized and justified her actions. She refused to admit she had done anything wrong. Still, the Holy Spirit would not let her go.

One day at church, the pastor spoke on betrayal. He talked about the betrayal Joseph endured when his own brothers sold him off as a slave, the betrayal Samson felt when the wife he loved sold him out to his enemies, and Jesus with the greatest betrayal of all. They all had one thing in common, they were all betrayed by their nearest and dearest.

Slowly, the wall she built around herself, leaving no place for a conscience, crumbled in the presence of God. It affected her powerfully not only in church but also at home, in her bedroom. She went on her knees and after God revealed the true state of her heart, she cried out for forgiveness.

Alice cut off her relationship with Tope without hesitation. She harbored no regrets about that decision. She could not blame her for the path she encouraged her to take. She felt she should have known better.

Though she finally repented with many tears, she knew that her actions had forever ruined a friendship that was once one of the best things that ever happened to her. Uzo had been more than a friend and she had tried to destroy her. That was unforgiveable.

A few months later, after that famous Facebook post, all of Lagos stood still for the wedding of Ugo Nwokedi and Uzo Madumere. The major news channels reported the event. They highlighted celebrities and financial bigwigs stepping out of their expensive vehicles and making their way into the Lagos Cathedral for the wedding ceremony.

Alice sat in her room and watched the proceedings on TV. She had received an invitation from Uzo but was too ashamed to respond. She sent a congratulatory message instead.

The camera taking aerial shots of the guests, zoomed down at the bride's arrival. As Uzo stepped out, Alice's mouth fell open. Uzo looked stunning! Whoever her stylist was, did an amazing job. She almost shimmered as she walked down the red carpet into the cathedral in a simple cut, off shoulder ivory dress that draped around her curves, accentuating only her best features. Uzo, in nobody's shadow today, was the star of the show.

"You deserve it all, friend," Alice whispered to the screen, and meant it.

Alice's eyes followed Uzo, her thoughts darting over who was walking her down the aisle and standing in as the bride's Father. When Alice realized who he was, her mouth fell open again. Uzo held the arms of the old Baba from the restaurant. Alice choked up at the sight; God did not leave Uzo fatherless on her wedding day. How people changed when money came into play. Baba looked nothing like a forgettable beggar by the side of the road anymore. He looked regal in his flowing *Agbada.* Looking every inch, the Father of the

Bride. He had cut his hair, his beard neatly trimmed. His smile was everything.

Alice looked closely, eager to find out the identity of the chief bridesmaid. There was none, and this broke her heart even more. Even after everything, Uzo would still not replace her, choosing to go on alone. It came again, the tightness in her chest, the darkness.

"Father forgive me, Uzo forgive me, Ugo forgive me." She fell on the floor of her room and rolled in anguish, begging for release. "Forgive me, Father, let them forgive me."

How can they give what you have not asked for?

"LORD, but I'm so ashamed."

"Yes."

Alice waited for more, but no other word came. She reached for her phone and searched for the message she had written the night after Uzo challenged her about misleading Ugo. In that message, she had acknowledged her wrong, admitted that jealousy and envy had consumed her, and begged for both their forgiveness. She ended by wishing them all God's best.

She never sent it. The darkness had been strong that night. It had tormented her about the potential disgrace and embarrassment she would incur if she apologized. That would mean she was conceding defeat. She had listened then, but today, the darkness was not there, and she saw an apology as the right thing to do. She quickly pressed send before she changed her mind. Once she did, a wave of peace washed over her.

"Thank you, my Lord. Thank you, Jesus." She rose, much lighter, and settled back to watch the wedding. She stayed glued to the screen, getting up only to use the bathroom or grab something to eat. When they announced them as husband and wife, she rejoiced with her friend and clapped alone in her apartment.

It was when they stood facing the crowd during thanksgiving that he caught her eye. The man standing beside Ugo. Alice crawled closer to the TV, put her hand on the screen and as if on cue, the cameraman zoomed in on the best man. Her body trembled.

"No, God, no."

Standing in his suit, a head taller than Ugo, was the most handsome man in the building. The same man she had seen in her dream. The man she had assumed was not real and relegated as a figment of her imagination, yet the one she silently measured every other man with. He wasn't supposed to be real, but there he was, standing right behind Ugo.

The irony of the whole situation came crashing around her. If she had only been happy for her friend, today she would have met her forever love, too. God had packaged her a blessing, but not the way she thought. He had wrapped it in Uzo's blessing.

"God, what have I done? What have I done to myself? I can't ask you to change it because I deserve it. I deserve it. I didn't even know he was real, but you kept and preserved him for me. And now I've ruined it by my own hand."

She cried till she was physically spent and fell asleep mouthing the words, "He is real."

Chapter Sixteen

SHE WAS STILL ASLEEP by eight o'clock that evening. Her phone buzzed and opened her eyes, looking around in a daze. The wedding must have been over because the TV station was back to their regular scheduled programing. She searched for her still buzzing phone.

She did not get too many calls lately and wondered who it could be. She finally found it under her chair, where it must have fallen after her revelation. All that happened before she slept came rushing back, but it surprised her to discover she no longer felt depressed about any of it. Yes, she had missed this blessing, but maybe God had another one in store for her. But even if he didn't, and she was to remain single all her life, it was going to be okay too.

Her phone was still ringing when she found it. On sighting the caller I.D, her heart raced. On her wedding day?

"Oh God, what do I say?" She felt that peace again and braved it. She picked up the phone.

"Hello" she said hesitantly. Her phone probably dialed hers by mistake. But it wasn't a mistake. Uzo's voice came through the handset and it felt like water on parched ground refreshing her soul.

"My friend. You should have been there!" She heard Uzo crying. Tears spilled down Alice's face, and she found it hard to speak.

"You should have been there beside me, Alice."

"I was too ashamed," she said finally. Both ladies were crying now at each end of the phone.

"I'm sorry. I can't even explain what came over me. I have never experienced such dark feelings before. I don't even recognize myself."

"Well," Uzo said sniffing loudly, "you still have one thing to do as my chief bridesmaid."

"What do you want me to do?" She checked her watch, thinking Uzo had an errand she needed help with.

"Come and collect my bouquet. If it's true that whoever catches it gets married next, then I want you to have it. I couldn't allow other people collect your blessing, could I?"

"Aww, Uzo. Where do you want me to pick it up from?"

"Pick it? Come downstairs and catch it, silly, Ugo and I are outside your house."

Alice had been sitting on the couch, she tumbled off it in her bid to get to the window. She saw them waving beside a black limousine still in their wedding attire, Uzo in her ivory dress and a handsome beaming Ugo beside her.

"Father, how can they be this kind to me?" Alice didn't bother taking the time to change into a more respectable outfit. She hurried downstairs in her pajamas, flew out of her door and both ladies ran into each other's arms. They held onto each other, sobbing. Alice kept begging for forgiveness and Uzo gave it, reassuring her friend over and over.

"You guys look so good together. I was watching, I didn't want to miss it." Alice wiped her face and rambled on, suddenly self-conscious in front of Ugo.

"I'm sorry, my farmer friend. You clean up nicely and you *fyne small sha.*"

"*See your big head, come here, joor.*" Ugo extended his own grace and embraced her warmly.

"Quickly, Alice, let's do this." Uzo bent over the rear seat of the car and brought out a gorgeous cascading bouquet. It perfectly complimented her simple, understated bridal look, "This is where I throw, and you catch."

Ugo shook his head and smiled at his wife indulgently. "Why don't you just hand it over to her and let's get going?"

"Noo! It doesn't work like that," Uzo insisted. "Alice, move back a bit."

Alice would have gone to the moon if she had asked her to. She took three steps back and waited. Uzo turned her back on her again and said a prayer loud enough for Alice to hear.

"I pray God will give you someone just perfect for you." She raised the bouquet over her head and flung it back. Alice didn't have far to go but had to stretch a little to catch it. Both ladies embraced and jumped around a while, causing an exasperated Ugo to cover his face with his palm. Another black SUV drove up and honked. The three adults all looked toward the car.

"Mr. and Mrs. Nwokedi, what are you guys playing at?" a weary voice called from the vehicle. Ugo and Uzo smiled.

From the driver's side, long legs slid out first, and then the rest of him followed. Suddenly, there he was walking towards them, smiling with pearly white teeth, his mustache neatly trimmed. The man in her dream.

"Oh, I'm sorry," he said when he spotted Alice, "I didn't realize they were with someone. I have been searching for the runaway couple for the past 30 minutes."

"I am sorry, Anthony," Uzo said and hugged him. "I just had to make this stop before we left. This is my best friend Alice, who couldn't make the wedding today."

Alice had no words. She could not believe he was here. She wanted to touch him, to feel that he was real.

"I heard of my missing partner," he said, giving her another dazzling smile. "Your friends here were a lot of work to keep under control, it would have been great to have you beside me."

"That is something I will regret for the rest of my life."

Alice realized from the way they were all staring at her she must have said it out loud. She looked around, looking for the nearest exit, but Ugo saved the day.

"Alice, meet my older brother Anthony."

"Brother?"

"Don't look so shocked. But I understand the surprise. We have different mums."

"Oh," Alice quickly processed this information since it answered the obvious. The dissimilarities between the two men were like night and day.

"Yeah," Anthony said, lightly punching Ugo's arm. "And also, we have different everything else too, tastes, interests, hobbies." Anthony smiled, now studying Alice more keenly.

"Yeah, that's why he abandoned us with the family business and went to New York to follow the money." Uzo laughed, returning the punch.

"Can you imagine me farming? I have no interest in how I get my food."

"As long as we get the food," Alice said at the same time as Anthony, both startling each other.

Uzo and Ugo laughed at them.

"Wow, synchronized sentencing, I have not seen that before." Uzo winked at Alice, who bowed and avoided looking at anyone.

"I am so sorry to break this party up, but my wife and I…" Ugo put his arms around Uzo's shoulders and pulled her close. Ugo waited for everyone to stop rolling their eyes. "I repeat, my WIFE and I have a three-month long-standing appointment that I am desperately eager to keep."

"*Ah ahn*, Ugo." Uzo pushed him away but couldn't hide her blush.

"Brother, we did not need to know that." Anthony covered his face with a palm.

"That's your business. Can we please leave now?" He pulled Alice into a hug. "Please, don't be a stranger, okay? We will be gone for two weeks, when we get back we must see."

"Thank you, Ugo. Can I text your wife within the two weeks?" Alice went over to hug Uzo. She did not want to cry but she felt like she was losing her friend after just having found her again.

"Never! Just forget you know her for now," he yelled as they got into the car.

Anthony stayed behind and shifted from one foot to another.

"Hey, Alice, once I am done exchanging the cars for these two, I'm kind of free for the evening. Would you mind if we went somewhere to… hang out?"

"Oh! I love hangouts!" Uzo yelled from her window.

"Of course, she can," Ugo said, poking his head through the window on Uzo's side of the car. "And Anthony, take her to a place called Love Legacy Cafe. I promise you, it's magical."

Only Anthony looked lost as the other three laughed. Alice waved enthusiastically as the car with the couple reversed out of her compound, leaving her alone with her dream man. She stepped back to take a proper look at him.

"What do you think? Should we try it? Are you up for it? I'll be back in an hour."

Everything was happening so fast. Alice wanted to stop time a minute so she could really absorb all that had taken place. He waited patiently for a reply. His eyes shone with eagerness. It worried Alice. He did not know her. He did not know the person she was or what she had done. Once he found out, she was sure the eagerness would fade. Maybe she should put a stop to it now, to avoid an even bigger disappointment later. But another thought crossed her mind. How many times do you get a chance to spend time with someone you have only met in a dream? Maybe for tonight, she would let herself feel the magic, knowing it would fade quickly.

"I'll be ready," she finally said.

He let out a slow breath and rubbed his hands together. A wide smile spread across his face. It sent a warmth to the bottom of Alice's stomach. "See you soon then."

As she carefully got ready for the outing, she prayed for the evening. Her feelings oscillated between excitement and dread. "Father, not my will, but yours. I want only what you want and no matter how the evening ends, help me be okay with it. In Jesus Name."

By the time he returned, her heart was at peace. It raced again when she saw him step out of the car. Alice decided not to get carried away and steered the conversation.

"Anthony, before we go further, I have something to tell you. It may be a deciding factor in how the rest of the evening goes, but I'd rather be honest."

She asked him to join her on the stairs outside her apartment building. He did and waited patiently for her to speak. She told him everything that had transpired between Ugo, Uzo and herself. She did not sugarcoat the events and took full responsibility for her role in the saga. She also told him of her journey into depression and God's saving grace. She shared about her renewed relationship with Christ and how her priorities now lay in pleasing Him as much as she could. Once she finished, she checked her watch. They had spent forty-five minutes together. Even though she did all the talking, she considered it a wonderful date. Her soul felt so free she wanted to sing. Talking about everything had been therapeutic.

He, on the other hand, had not said a word throughout her narration. He remained silent even after she finished. She did not think he would stay after all she told him, so she stood up. He stood as well.

"So how do we get to this extra special cafe?" His deep baritone was even deeper in the quiet of the evening.

Alice stared. "Didn't you hear what I said about trying to sabotage your brother and your sister- in- law's relationship?"

"I did, Alice, and I also heard of your repentance. Ugo and Uzo seem to have no problem with you, and they are the ones involved. So can we go now?"

Alice nodded. Emotion welled up, but she pushed it back. Sobbing uncontrollably may not be a good look for a first date. She kept thinking how unreal it was. He had not rejected her. She told him everything, and he was still here.

She walked towards the car, deep in thought when she felt a hand gently pull her back. Anthony turned her around to face him.

"Thank you for telling me. Even if I knew nothing else about you, I know this, you are honest, and I really value that in a friend."

Alice smiled but could not speak still. He called her a friend. Her eyes glowed.

"I hope you will allow me to return the favor by letting me share with you all the gory details of my life before my conversion last year. But I think I should get you to the restaurant first. I am afraid you'll refuse to go out with me once I am done."

Now, Alice laughed hard at that, and she did not bolt at the restaurant. Instead, they stayed talking till the servers had to let them know they were ready to close. They left Love Legacy Cafe holding hands and laughing.

From his usual position at the car park, the old man, known as Baba, sat and waited. When he saw the couple approach, he looked to the heavens.

"Lord, what would you like me to tell them?"

The End

About The Author

More of OGUGUA AJAYI at

www.ogugua-ajayi.com

www.ingramcontent.com/pod-product-compliance
Lightning Source LLC
Chambersburg PA
CBHW061530050726
47593CB00002B/749